CW00376832

# Grin

## By
## Stuart Keane

To Jenny

All The Best!

When the blood and guts bits aren't happening, you look for a bit of a break to get your breath back but with *Grin*, the relaxing bits are the psychological horror bits that just turn your mind upside down and inside out.

So, I didn't expect this but my god this has introduced me to Stuart Keane's work in a fantastic way. I have to say he doesn't write like he seems as a person on Facebook and such like. He seems a fairly decent chap. Until he writes.

He is one of those authors that I put into the easy category. What I mean by that is that you slide into the book very easily. It doesn't take you long before you feel totally at ease with what you are reading. You feel as if you have known the characters for a long time after only a few pages. It flows extremely well and is paced perfectly for the different types of horror featured in the story. It has blood when it needs it and emotion in abundance in both the bloody parts and the head feck parts.

So after not reading Mr Keane's work before, I understand I have a bit of catching up to do. For that, I am very excited because after getting a flavour of how he can write, I am now convinced that I have some wonderful stuff ahead of me.

5* Review of Grin
Nev Murray, Confessions of a Reviewer

"Stuart Keane has taken the baton from Shaun Hutson, in the race for British horror gold."

"A remarkable writer, and a brilliant story teller."

"Keane might only be a newcomer to the writing scene in terms of published output, but already he exhibits that he has the writing chops and skillset to turn out some exemplary material."

"Keane is a horror writer that shouldn't be missed."

"Stuart – clearly a student of the late great Richard Laymon – has an keen sense for what makes horror such an entertaining and enthralling genre, and he understands that the story will hit all the harder if the reader can relate."

Reviews courtesy of Amazon.com/Amazon.co.uk

Also by
Stuart Keane

Available on Amazon Kindle and Print


<u>Author</u>

The Customer is Always…
Charlotte
All or Nothing
Whispers – Volume 1: A Collection
Cine
Whispers –Volume 2: A Second Collection

<u>Author/Editor</u>

Carnage: Extreme Horror
(With Jack Rollins, Kyle M. Scott and Angel Gelique)

<u>Editor</u>

Undead Legacy

Copyright © Stuart Keane 2015
Cover art copyright © Mark Kelly 2015
Published: January 26, 2016
Publisher: Stuart Keane

The right of Stuart Keane to be identified as author of this Work has
been asserted by him in accordance the Copyright, Designs and
Patents Act 1988.

All rights reserved.
This book is copyright material and must not be copied, reproduced,
transferred, distributed, leased, licensed or publicly performed or
used in any way except as specifically permitted in writing by the
publishers, as allowed under the terms and conditions under which
it was purchased or as strictly permitted by applicable copyright
law. Any unauthorised distribution or use of this text may be a
direct infringement or the author's and publisher's rights and those
responsible may be liable in law accordingly.


'Grin' is a work of fiction. Names, characters, businesses,
organizations, places, events, and incidents either are the product of
the author's imagination or are used fictitiously. Any resemblance
to actual persons, living or dead, events, or locales is entirely
coincidental. For more information about the artist, please visit

For more information about the author, please visit
www.stuartkeane.com

For more information about the artist, please visit
www.zgrimv.com

To visit the Confessions of a Reviewer Website, please visit
www.confessionsofareviewer.blogspot.co.uk

# Acknowledgements

Once again, I want to thank Neil for editing Grin. Efficient and precise, and not too angry at my tight deadlines, you came through again, which is the sign of an excellent editor. Thank you!

I want to thank Peggy Howes, Kindra Sowder, Doug Rinaldi and Lewis Gilson. Often on Facebook, I will invite readers to feature in my work, and these amazing people helped me out massively. When creating a story, some things can unexpectedly pop up – in this case, a particularly nasty scene with plenty of people – and having a handful of original names certainly comes in handy when this is the case. The end of this book took me by surprise, so thank you for being on hand.

A special, appreciative thank you to Nicky Barrett and Richard D. Ramsey. As you are about to find out, the 'grin' of the title is a horrific wound to receive. To ensure total accuracy, Nicky and Richard – who both work in the medical field – provided me with crucial information on the treatment of such wounds, with rehabilitation times and specific procedures explained to me in depth. It was a huge, rewarding, learning experience. A massive thank you to you guys. Without your expertise, this book would have taken a lot longer to nail down.

As usual, thank you to Stephen King, Richard Laymon, James Herbert, Shaun Hutson, and Clive Barker for putting me on the right path to horror fiction. Without them, I doubt I would be doing this.

Finally, I wish to thank my readers, many of whom I talk to, chat with and communicate with online. You're the reason I write, so never forget that. Feel free to get in touch on Facebook, Twitter or my website www.stuartkeane.com.

Enjoy!

For my beautiful sisters, Joanne and Kirsty.
Two of the strongest women I know. For any author, that's true
inspiration.

# PART ONE

## Consequences

# ONE

"You know the score, right?"

"Yep."

"Positive?"

"Yep."

"You'd better be sure. If you fuck this up, there'll be hell to pay."

"For fuck sake, Ross, I got it, okay?" Dennis snatched the briefcase from his boss and inhaled, breathing in the chilled, evening air. "Why don't you trust me?"

"Because you're a fucking liability, that's why. Do we need to go over your past?" Ross Rhodes tensed up, preparing for a confrontation. Dennis noticed and backed down, sagging in the shoulders, bowing to the alpha male. He cracked a fake smile.

"No, no need."

"Good, because I fucking own you. *Own you!* Got that? I say jump, you say pretty please and how fucking high with a cherry on top, got it?"

Dennis nodded. A prickly rage was building inside of him, burning through his veins. Again, the fake smile stretched across his face. "Got it. Loud and clear."

Rhodes walked around to the passenger door of the idling Audi beside him.

Dennis backed up a step, smiled, and held a hand up in gesture. "Don't worry, Ross. I got this."

Rhodes said nothing, grunted, and ducked into the vehicle. The door closed with a soft clunk and the car pulled away quietly. Within seconds, it disappeared from the alley onto the street.

Dennis breathed out and rested on a small brick wall behind him. He placed the briefcase on the crumbling concrete beneath his feet and realised he was sweating. Removing a handkerchief from his pocket, he wiped the perspiration from his brow.

A door opened behind him, squeaking on the silent night air, and a man dressed in grimy white clothes appeared. The new arrival took a few steps into the alley and sparked up a cigarette. His attention wandered for a moment, taking in the scenery, before settling on Dennis. His eyes narrowed and he exhaled a plume of smoke. "You okay, pal?"

Dennis stopped rubbing his brow, glanced around and smiled, more in relief than anything else. "Sure, I'm fine."

"Long day?"

"You could say that," Dennis said, chuckling to himself.

"Want a smoke?" The man held out the packet to him.

"No, I quit. Not sure why…but I did."

"Good on ya, bro. I couldn't give these bad boys up; I'd be a raving mess if I did."

Dennis casually observed the man. He noticed the messy whites and black and white striped trousers. A tight, food stained apron was wrapped around his waist. His fingers were thick and knotted and as the chef stepped into the glare of the streetlight, several scars – emphasised by darker flecks of skin – were obvious.

The pieces fell into place and Dennis grinned. "You a chef, huh?"

The newcomer nodded. "Seven years, straight out of cookery school. I tell you, man, I wouldn't have done it if I knew it was going to be this stressful. Not worth a fuckin' jot."

Dennis straightened up and stretched his neck; a loud crack resonated down the empty alleyway. He groaned.

The chef blew out another stream of smoke and watched him. "You should get that checked."

Dennis collected the suitcase and ambled over. "I know. Any hints? For stress relief, I mean. I hear you guys have the worst job in the world. Stress wise and all that."

"Not really, no. Well, you could start smoking again?"

Dennis chuckled. "Sure, why not. One won't kill me."

The chef held out the pack of Marlboros. Dennis pinched the exposed filter from the end of the pack and slid it out, placing it between his dry lips. The chef pocketed the smokes and lifted a Zippo lighter. He flicked the lid and ignited the device in one swift swipe, a sound that echoed around them. The small flame danced in the evening chill as it lit the cigarette between Dennis' lips. He sucked in a lungful, held for a few seconds, and breathed out. The smoke caressed his throat and escaped through his mouth and nostrils with a long, deep sigh. His eyes closed. "My God, I forgot how good that shit is."

The chef nodded. "Two hundred covers a day. Smoking is essential, man."

Dennis moved over and sat on the wall beside the chef, who was leaning on an open dumpster. The essence of old rubbish and decaying food hung in the air. A silence settled over them as Dennis checked his watch. "It's half past ten. I assume your shift is finished?"

"Yep, cleaning down time. Well, in due course."

"Waiting for the last customers to leave?"

"You got it. Every night, I tell the line cooks to leave the line for half an hour. Clean down the rest of the kitchen, but leave the line. All you need is a strung-out waitress bringing a plate in and tripping or slamming it down. Food everywhere. Cleaning the line twice is a waste of labour. Therefore, I wait. Makes perfect sense. The other line cooks label the foods and tidy. I come out for a well-earned smoke."

The chef toked once again, finishing the cigarette. "Anyway, how did you know?"

"I used to be a waiter. You learn the trade and routines pretty quickly."

"You work in London?"

"No, up north." Dennis pointed to the sky with his cigarette.

"Anywhere big?"

"Not really. Couple of seafood places, the odd TGI Friday's, nothing as fancy as…" Dennis glanced up at the back of the restaurant, looking for a hint to the establishment's name. He saw bare, crumbling red bricks and steam billowing from a crooked funnel embedded beneath a dark window.

"Where am I?"

The chef laughed. "Mamma Sue's. Italian."

"You don't look Italian?"

"Shhh, don't tell anyone." The chef smiled and stubbed out his cigarette on the wall. "I'm trained Italian, not born it. I still make the best pasta in Soho, though."

"I'll take that as a recommendation."

"And a secret. If Joe Magniello at Pirlo's found out, he'd have me killed." He smiled and slapped his thighs. "Just jokin', Joe knows I love him."

"I've been to Pirlo's…decent place. Great lasagna."

"You haven't eaten here yet."

"Maybe I have," Dennis nodded.

An awkward silence settled on them. The chef pushed away from the dumpster and stood up straight. "I'll book you a table if you want?"

"Nah, it's okay. I don't know when I'll be in town next." Dennis met his eyes, not flinching.

The chef smiled uneasily and tensed.

He looked up and down the alleyway and started towards the back door. "Nice meeting you."

"Likewise. Thanks for the smoke."

Dennis held his half-finished cigarette in the air. He watched the chef go, observing him.

The chef trotted up the steps, took one final look back, and disappeared through the white door. It closed on its latch with a thud and bounced back, still open. Ease of exit for removal of furniture and rubbish. Dennis recalled the many late nights as a kitchen porter. Remembered bringing out wet bags of waste and refuse, spilling bin juice all over his new Nikes. The stench of fat and fish that ruined many of his clothes.

*We all started somewhere.*

Dennis dropped the cigarette onto the floor and stamped it out. His smile disappeared as he glanced up and down the alleyway, imitating the chef from moments before. He saw several fissures of steam and heard little noise coming from the streets of London beyond.

Dennis was alone.

He pulled two slim leather gloves from his pocket and slid them on.

Dennis eased his hand behind him, beneath his suit jacket and removed a silenced Beretta. The material of the coat made a slight swishing noise on his gloves. He twisted the muzzle – firmly attached. He tucked it under his arm and did the same with a second, identical Beretta. Both ready, both loaded with sixteen 9mm parabellum rounds. After a quick check, each firearm had a bullet in the chamber.

Dennis clicked the safety off on both firearms. He slid one into his belt and breathed out.

"Please God; keep me safe in this time of need."

Dennis walked towards the doorway.

His brain processed vital information within seconds. The chef had mentioned cleaning down took half an hour, which meant the line cooks would be either cleaning right now, or already finished, thus vacating the kitchen. Unless there was another alley or room to smoke in, the chef would have shared his smoke with several colleagues.

Most kitchens only had one back door.

Dennis knew a kitchen of this size required seven line cooks, maybe eight including a prep chef, nine for dessert too, unless they doubled up the tasks. Worst case, nine people, ten including the head chef. The wait staff would be in the dining room, turning over tables, cleaning cutlery, taking tips.

Customers would be few, probably inebriated; maybe one or two forcefully removed.

He reached the top step and listened, his ear against the wooden surface. After a second, he stepped to the side as the door swung outwards. A pot washer, indicated by his white t-shirt and lack of chef whites, stumbled before Dennis, tripping over the outstretched, unexpected leg before him.

Dennis shot the newcomer in the back of the head.

A solid *whup* disappeared in the heavy silence of the alleyway. The pot washer's face exploded outwards, splattering the floor and steps below him with dark blood. Several fragments of bone tinkered on the concrete. Before the victim could go any further, Dennis kicked him sideways into the open dumpster. The dead body toppled onto some rubbish bags with a solid whoosh. Rubbish flew up into the air as the body came to a rest, souring the air even more. Dennis leaned over, shot him in the head again, and closed the dumpster lid.

Nine remaining.

Maybe.

Dennis pulled the door, gun ahead of him, and entered Mamma Sue's.

The kitchen, vast and metallic, stood before him. Every work surface was silver, sparkling, and spotless. Dennis stood in a shadowy alcove, tucked into a dark recess, away from the food preparation areas. Quickly scanning the room, he noticed no movement. No one was present. The normal bustle of the kitchen; shouting, clinking of plates and food hissing, were all absent. A dull murmur of customer conversation emanated from a doorway opposite him. Shadows danced behind a misted, circular glass window.

The chef from before walked in front of Dennis, not noticing the intruder, his attention elsewhere. He stopped at a counter and starting placing some knives on a magnetized strip on the wall. Methodical metal thuds occurred as the blades found their home.

Dennis waited.

The chef took a minute to finish the task. He lifted a red cutting board from the surface below him, spun it in the air, and slid in into a groove beneath the surface. He then leaned on the counter, stretching his muscles. A huge sigh escaped from deep down, the noise of a weary worker.

Still no other kitchen staff.

They were alone.

Dennis took this as his cue.

He smirked and silently stepped forward. Emerging from the shadows like a silent demon of death, he raised the Beretta. "You know smoking kills, right?"

The chef paused for a second, and then spun around. Recognition in his eyes betrayed him, made him hesitate. Before he could utter a word, Dennis fired four silent rounds into his chest and one into his face, which imploded in a mist of blood and obliterated skull. Blood sprayed from his bullet holes, spattering the metal surfaces and floor. The chef gasped and groaned, falling and spinning backwards. Soggy squelching filled the silence as red fluid pumped from the man's dying body. His face collided hard with a metal surface, sending various utensils to the floor in a cacophony of clattering.

Dennis backed away into the shadows and left the kitchen.

He leapt down the steps, turned left and exited the alleyway. As he went, he dropped the magazines from his guns into his palms, pocketed them and slid the empty weapons back into his waistband. He collected the briefcase as he walked away.

He was on the street before the first terrified screams pierced the chilly, night air. A moment later, he climbed into his waiting BMW and drove away.

# TWO

"How was school today?"

"Really cool! We got to chop up a sheep's heart."

"Ugh, that's gross."

"Not gross, it's sick! So cool!"

Dani smiled at her younger brother, bemused by his morbid curiosity. The red school bus – a wheezing, chugging behemoth – pulled away behind them. Dark, acrid smoke filled the air, making Dani cough. She waved a hand in front of her face as Teddy skipped ahead on the cracked pavement, full of energy and youthful abandon. His rucksack slapped his back as he twirled and danced. Dani stopped coughing and frowned. "Did you have a Coke for lunch?"

"Yeah, of course, duh! I had *two* cans! Why?"

"You know that stuff is bad for you."

"Yeah well, one won't hurt."

"If Mum finds out, you're in trouble."

"You gonna tell her? *Dobber, dobber, dobber!*"

Dani smiled. "Teddy, calm down. I'm not going to *dob* you in. You'd better take it easy though, or she'll figure it out for herself." She thought about it. "Actually, carry on; you might as well wear yourself out."

"Wooo."

Teddy spun around a rusted lamppost, his trainers scraping on the concrete, his small frame twirling down to the ground before bouncing back up.

Dani smirked, thinking she'd seen that in an old movie once, and removed her mobile phone from her pocket.

No text messages and no calls.

Slipping the device back into her pocket, she gazed across the street. Several children were returning from the school day; walking in couples and groups. The occasional child was alone, the familiar string of headphones draping their chest. Groups convened on street corners. Some were laughing. Others, accompanied by street-cred crippling parents, looked at the ground as they ambled home, ashamed by their accomplices. The street, otherwise, was quiet. The occasional car drove by. In the distance, a train clacked through the local station, not stopping, heading to an unknown destination.

Distracted, Dani didn't see Teddy speed along the pavement. He plowed into her midriff, knocking her sideways, and sent himself toppling to the dusty pavement. Dani straightened her jacket and groaned. "For God *sake*, Teddy! Get up."

"You took the Lord's name in vain!"

"Yeah, so fucking sue me. *Up!*"

"You said a swear!"

"Don't get me started."

Dani was no longer smiling, irritated, wanting to get home. She grabbed her brother by the arm and hoisted him to his feet. She brushed him down with her coat sleeves, not wanting to ruin her nails, and patted him on the shoulder. "Let's go, Mum's making dinner. It's your favourite tonight, a picnic!"

Teddy's eyes widened and lit up. He towed the line, falling in beside his sister.

He gazed up at Dani, his green eyes narrowing with childlike innocence. For a moment, he said nothing, taking in his sister's attire. Under her leather jacket, she wore a crinkled, blue chamois blouse, assembled with a mid-thigh black skirt and a pair of white trainers.

The brightness of the trainers accentuated her tanned, smooth legs. Today, a ponytail dangled over her left shoulder, flapping in the breeze.

Teddy knew his sister was pretty because she had a boyfriend. Only pretty girls got boyfriends. But, to him, she was his *sister*. She had girl cooties. Anyway, he preferred the woman on Nickelodeon; *she* was pretty. He looked up at Dani again. "Why don't you go to school?"

Dani glanced down and continued looking forward. "Me? You know why."

"Everyone goes to school. David told me that everyone has to, or the police go to your house and arrest your parents."

Dani chortled. "That's not strictly true. Anyway, I finished school, I go to college now."

"What's college?"

"Grown up school. For older people."

"How old are you?"

"Don't you know this?"

"I forgot. I'm just a kid, *remember*?"

Dani chuckled. "Seventeen. A whole nine years older than you." Dani tapped her brother on the tip of his nose. "I finished school a year ago."

"I can't wait to finish school. I want to cut up more sheep's hearts."

"So you want to be a butcher?"

"What?"

"Never mind." Dani walked for a few steps and they arrived outside Kambo's, the local corner shop. The smell of baked goods and candy piqued her interest. Dani looked across the street and saw their house. Her Dad's black BMW was parked in the driveway.

*He's home early*, she thought.

"Can I get some sweets?"

Dani said nothing for a second, distracted by her Dad's potential presence, and turned to Teddy. "Sorry, what did you say?"

"Can I get some sweets?"

*Good idea*, she thought. *Hide the fact he had Coke. The better of two evils.* "Yes, you got your pocket money?"

"A whole two whole pounds. I'm rich!"

Dani smiled. "Go on then. Be quick, moneybags."

Teddy pushed into the shop door, the bell ringing as it spun inwards. Dani glanced into the store and saw Mr. Kambo behind the counter. He shot her a dirty look, as if to say *'mind your fucking kid.'* Dani sneered and looked away.

She took her phone from her pocket. Again, no text messages.

*What was he playing at?*

"Dani!"

She turned around and saw Ben approaching. Relief washed over her and she grinned, opening her arms for a hug. Ben scooped her into his muscular arms, squeezed her gently and swung her around. After two spins, he placed Dani back down and kissed her softly. Their lips mashed, tongues flicking against one another. She pulled away, blushing. "You scared me. I've been checking my phone all day."

Ben smirked. "Sorry, my battery died. I thought I'd pop over and see you instead. Can't have you missing me too much, how would you cope?"

"Yeah, I think I'd be okay. There are plenty of other handsome boys to date." Dani playfully punched Ben, knocking him back a little. Secretly, she missed him like crazy. A warm feeling of happiness spread throughout her. She cuddled into his muscular arm.

"What are you up to tonight?"

"Dinner with the folks." Dani glanced at her house again, the BMW sinking her stomach somewhat. "Dad's home tonight so I don't think I can get away."

"You sure?"

"I don't know, Ben. I'll let you know, okay. What you *can* do is charge your bloody phone."

"I will when I get home."

"Good. If not tonight, we can hang out tomorrow?"

"I had a nice romantic evening planned for you too. Candlelit dinner, some wine and…well, you know."

"I do know. I told you, not until I'm ready. I want it to special."

"Not too long I hope. A man can only wait so long…"

"If you love me, you'll wait as long as it takes."

Ben went to reply, but said nothing. Dani raised an eyebrow. "You *will* wait, right? I said I didn't want to rush this. Respect that, okay?"

Ben nodded. "Sure thing, snugglebum."

Dani blushed bright red and looked around. "Not in public…"

Teddy ran past and swatted his sister on the rump. "Snugglebum? My *God*, get me a puke bucket, *urghhhhh*!" He stuck a finger in his mouth and pretended to vomit. Dani looked up at Ben and scowled. "See what you did?"

Ben chuckled. "I'll see you later…snugglebum." He chuckled, leaned in and kissed her on the lips. She sighed, closing her eyes. His lips tasted of Juicy Fruit chewing gum, the sweet flavour made her smile. Ben pulled away and walked down the street, back the way they'd come. She watched him go. A sense of loss began to spread through her heart.

Dani turned towards her house. Teddy was opening the front gate.

"I hope you looked both ways before crossing the road, you little shit." Dani walked quickly across the road, took a cautious look at the BMW and entered her house.

\*\*\*\*\*

Detective Inspector Scott sighed, a plume of grey cigarette smoke escaping his chapped lips. He scratched his forehead with the butt of his palm and groaned. He stared at the yellow crime scene tape in the dark, dingy alleyway and closed his eyes.

Rain fell on the floor beside him with an infinitely patient pitter-patter. The crime scene tape flapped loudly in the breeze, poking at the migraine forming at the base of his skull.

It was his night off. He'd been sharing drinks with his girlfriend at the local nightclub. Date night, she called it, which, in some relationship binding way, meant he was obligated to attend. They did it twice a month, mostly on weekends. This time, it fell on a Wednesday. Tanya said it showed they were in love and it meant the relationship wasn't growing stale. He believed it; they'd been together six years.

A miracle in his opinion.

She mentioned the six years too, like making a subtle but obvious point. That's when he necked the first whiskey. He loved spending quality time with the woman, sure, but her need to label everything irked him. Before she got her next sentence out – as she examined the complicated layout of her red and orange cocktail, complete with umbrella, curly straw and strawberry décor – he necked his second. She talked about her day, her career, how things were going. A promotion had occurred, which he remembered her mentioning a while ago, but absently forgot until it became a topic of conversation. Then she asked him about his job before realising it was a no go. Classified information. He couldn't discuss his job. Which made him the silent one in this relationship.

It didn't do him any favours.

"Maybe we can catch a movie after this? The new Sandra Bullock movie is out."

He necked his third whiskey.

"You're very quiet tonight, something the matter?"

"No, just…well, I'm not in the mood. Long day."

"I'm sorry. We can leave if you want?"

"No, it's fine. You shouldn't ruin your evening for me."

He wanted to walk out and go home, shut off his phone, and slump on the sofa with a cold beer and some chicken wings.

He wanted to scream it in her face.

She didn't deserve that. She deserved the best, more than he could give.

Therefore, he remained quiet and half-smiled, counting his lucky stars that he had someone so beautiful and understanding. Radiant brunette hair, sparkling cerulean eyes, a face that could adorn any fashion magazine in the world, and *that* smile, the one that melted his cold dead heart. She loved him for whatever bizarre reason and he regretted it every day. The danger involved in his job could ruin her life at any moment.

"You're not ruining my evening, honey. This is our evening; we can do whatever you want to do. Name it." The sparkle was present in those amazing orbs, as always. He couldn't help but smile.

Scott necked his fourth whiskey and realised he'd only been at the club an hour. His drinking pace startled him. Scott said nothing, staring into the empty tumbler before him. His eye caught a reflection of Tanya in the glass. She was gazing at him, concerned, her face twisted like the result of some funfair mirror experiment.

"I'm fine here. Seriously," he lied.

"I'll get us another." She smiled and scooped up the empty glasses. As she walked to the bar, he watched her go, her rump caressed by the tight dress that ended at the top of her silky thighs. Her long, bronze legs flexed as she crossed the dance floor with poise and elegance. Her brunette hair flapped and waved on her back. Scott observed the men around her, their gazes pulled from their drinks and their own girlfriends by her presence. He saw the scornful looks on the female faces too, and smiled for the third time that evening.

That's when he got the call.

*Shit*, he thought.

*Why didn't I turn off my phone?*

After a long thirty seconds, he swiped the screen and answered. "Scott."

"Scott, its Davidson. We need you to take the crime scene in Soho. The Italian restaurant with the homicide."

"Mamma Sue's? I thought Jarrett was on it?"

"Apparently he has the flu, the pussy can't come in today. Besides, we can't have him coughing and spluttering all over the evidence. I want you on it. I know it's your day off but hey, we don't get days off. You in?"

"Do I have a choice?"

"That's the spirit."

Davidson hung up. Scott pulled the phone from his ear and grunted, putting it back in his pocket. As if perfectly timed, Tanya returned with their drinks. She saw the look on his face and groaned. "Work called, didn't they?"

"Yep."

"It's your day off."

"I don't get days off...not really," he said, mimicking his Sergeant's words.

"Great. Just great."

"I'll make it up to you, I promise. On Saturday, we can catch that film...the one with Sandra Bullock in it."

Tanya's eyes widened. "Really? You *hate* her movies."

"I know...but I love you more."

*Man, I can be soppy.*

Tanya leaned in for a kiss, a soft, lingering kiss that gave Scott all the pep he needed to get over to Soho. "Come on, let's get a cab home, I need to change out of this shirt."

An hour later, Scott was outside Mamma Sue's.

He finished his cigarette and tossed it in a puddle beside him. The butt sizzled as it hit the surface. The rain was easing up a little; the pitter-patter was ebbing and less noticeable. Scott shoved a stick of gum in his mouth and shook his head. The dull ache was more a throb now.

*Damn that glorious whisky.*

He stepped forward, ducking under the crime scene tape. The stench of death was ever-present, a normal occurrence for this part of London.

# THREE

The credits rolled on the silent black and white movie.

Dani scooted up from her elbows, shuffled onto her rump and turned around. Her father was sleeping in his armchair, his mouth wide open, a sliver of drool on his chin. Dani grinned and silently crept up on him, her slipper-clad feet inaudible on the plush, new carpet. As she neared him, his left eye opened and he smiled.

"Damn, you're good," she said, chuckling.

"No one can sneak up on me." His hands shot out, tickling his daughter, making her squeal in laughter. Dani's mother, Carla, walked into the room. She was stirring some mashed potatoes in a bowl. "What is going…oh, okay." Dani ran across the living room and stopped at the foot of the stairs, her face red with exertion. Dennis stopped halfway across the room, a wide grin on his face. He walked over to Carla, wiped the drool from his chin, and planted a kiss on her cheek. "Dinner ready?"

"Almost. Dani, call your brother." She returned to the kitchen. *"Teddy! Dinner!"*

Muted thuds sounded on the hallway floor above. Seconds later, he appeared on the stairs, taking them two at a time. Dani blocked his way. She deepened her voice and jutted out her jaw. "A *pound* to pass."

"What are you, a troll?"

"Yes, a troll with a toll."

"Get outta my way, jooker. Teddy ducked under his sister's outstretched arm and ran to the dining room. Dani smiled. *Jooker. She always wondered where that endearing nickname had originated.*

She chuckled and followed her brother into the kitchen.

The square dining table held a huge spread of food. Chicken, sliced into many different shapes, mashed potato, gravy, peas, broccoli, and Yorkshire puddings. Two bottles of wine, one red and one white, sat at the head of the table, in front of Dennis. A six-pack of Coke sat at the other end. Carla walked in and placed a pot of redcurrant sauce on the table, completing the meal. Teddy took his normal seat and Dani sat opposite him.

"This looks great, Mum," Dani enthused. "I love picnic night," she said excitedly, looking in her brother's direction.

"Yeah, amazing. Look at this spread!" Teddy's eyes were wide in wonder as he surveyed the platter in front of him and met his sister's gaze.

Dennis coughed. "Teddy, care to say grace?"

Teddy put his hands together. He took a deep breath. "Rub a dub gosh, thanks for the nosh."

The entire family laughed. The scent of the food made Dani's mouth water. The essence of roasted chicken and the wonderful, stocky scent of gravy permeated the cheerful, homely air. Dennis popped the red wine, pouring himself a glass. The alcoholic twang of wine joined the feast of aromas in the room. Carla sat down and Dennis tinkled his glass. "I know we normally don't say grace, but I wanted to tonight."

"Dad, it's getting coooold," Teddy whined, half-mockingly.

Dani and Carla sat silent, allowing Dennis to continue.

"I've come to realise that, despite my short-comings, I have the best family a man can ask for. I have a smart-arse son who excels in football and has the same sharp tongue I did at his age, and a clever daughter who's just started college.

I never went to college, I didn't have the privilege, and I'm so proud that you did. I also have a beautiful wife, the woman who gave me two of the finest children in the world. For everything, I'm truly grateful."

Dennis held his glass in the air, silently. Carla handed a Coke to Dani and Teddy, who raised their cans in unison. "Cheers."

Dennis smiled. "Let's eat."

Carla started dishing out the dinner. Dani passed a plate of creamy mashed potatoes to her father. Teddy took a huge swig of his Coke. Dennis eyed him as he scooped the potatoes onto his plate. "You go easy on that stuff; I don't want you bouncing off the ceilings."

"I won't, Dad."

"You won't what?"

"Bounce off the ceilings. They're too high anyway."

Dennis grinned and ruffled his son's hair.

Dani poured some gravy onto her chicken, circling her plate. "Mom, can you pass the broccoli?"

"Sure, hon."

After a few moments, the family had their choice of food. Carla looked around the table. "Enjoy everyone. There's plenty more to go around."

The family tucked into their dinner.


"That was a wonderful dinner, Mum. Thank you."

"My pleasure, honey." Carla was washing up the plates, dipping them into a bowl of soapy water, scrubbing them with a cloth, and passing them to Dani - who was on drying duty. The youngest woman was piling the crockery on the side, ready to put away.

"How was college today?"

"It was okay, nothing special. Theory in Media is a little boring. Besides, the teacher has no control over the students. Half don't turn up and when they do, they completely disrespect him.

It's a little sad. Sometimes…well, you don't need to hear this."

"No, go on. I like hearing about my daughter, the *student*. It's so *glamourous*."

Dani smiled. "Well, I feel sorry for the guy. Sometimes he teaches three or four people only. The other students are too busy at the pub or dossing in the games room. It's no way to earn a living."

"Yeah, but think of it his way. *You're* still learning. One kid, twelve kids, it doesn't matter. You're a good student, you pay attention and you'll come out of this smelling like roses. Fuck the other kids."

"*Mum!*"

"Well…if they can't respect their education, then *fuck* them indeed."

Dani chuckled. "I suppose you're right…fuck them."

"Ah, ah, ah, money in the swear jar, now."

"But Mum, you *just…*"

"I'm a grown up." Carla held her daughters gaze for a second and laughed. "Just kidding. Not a word of this to your father or brother."

"Deal." Dani picked up a stack of plates and slid them into a cupboard below the worktop. She closed the door, clipping her finger. "Ow, *fuck.*"

"You okay, honey?"

"Yeah, just clipped my…"

"*Swear jar!*"

Both women spun around and saw Teddy standing in the doorway. Dani sucked her finger and Carla placed her hands on her hips, exasperated. He ran away, bouncing across the carpet to the stairs. They could hear him as he went. "Swear jar, swear jar, Mom and Dani dropped a *swear!*"

Dani smiled. "No more Coke for him then."

Carla nodded, turned and emptied the sink.

"Little shit," she muttered, under her breath.

Dani chuckled.

Two hours later, Teddy's rasping snores resonated through the crack in his bedroom door. Dennis smiled, closing his son's door slowly. He snapped the upstairs hallway light off and walked to this daughter's room, knocking gently on the pink door. "Yes," came a muted voice. Dennis pushed the door open with a scarred knuckle by instinct – no fingerprints - and walked into the room.

Dani was sitting on her bed, legs crossed, typing away on her pink laptop. The blue glow illuminated her face as her brown eyes, full of concentration and guile, stared at the screen. Dennis gazed around the room and grinned.

Over the years, the room has gone from a kid's domain with pictures of ponies and cartoons, to posters of the latest pop stars, X Factor rejects, or whatever movie hunk was popular that month. Now, artwork adorned the walls, the shelves devoid of Lego and replaced with module books and research material. Dennis never really understood his daughter, but he'd raised her on family values and as a result, she had a deep sense of discipline and respect. He trusted his daughter to put family and career before anything else, including boys, and he was one of the few fathers who knew his daughter would honour that.

He smiled, proud.

Dennis gazed at Dani, her pink pyjama legs riding her calves to reveal dark, olive skin, a gene from his own family tree. Her white t-shirt only contrasted against her smooth arms, again dark with an Italian heritage; one he rarely discussed but knew existed. Her hair was in a towel, a single wet lock hung over her left ear, damp from a recent shower. The smell of her candy shower gel, a recent birthday present, still lingered in the air.

Dani looked up, still typing. "Hey, Dad."

"Hey."

"Everything alright?"

"Yeah, just saying goodnight. It's been a long day."

"Night." Dani broke eye contact and returned to her work.

Dennis gulped, but didn't move. Dani, aware of his presence, continued typing. "What?"

"I'm so proud of you," Dennis said, feeling a little foolish. He walked into the room and sat on the edge of the bed. "You know that, don't you?"

"Sure." Dani smiled. She looked up at her father. The radiance from her innocent smile sent a warm tremble of pride through Dennis's heart. "I know you are, Dad, you tell me all the time."

"Well, it's because I am. So much."

"And I'm proud of you."

"Why?"

"For bringing me and doucheface up."

"Your brother's name is Teddy."

"Yeah, that's what I said, doucheface." Dani chuckled. "You brought us up; you married the coolest woman in the world. You have reason to be proud too. I know people whose parents combined didn't possess one parental gene. You're awesome, Dad."

"Good. I'm glad you know that."

"I do."

A silence settled between them. Dennis stood up, kissed Dani on the forehead and walked away. He paused, turned back and held out his hand. "Here, I want you to have this."

Dani looked up, frowning. "What is it?"

"It's my key. To the BMW."

"What?"

"I got a spare made. I want you to learn how to drive…at some point. When you pass, the car is yours."

"Seriously? You're *giving* me a BMW?" Dani took the black fob with the blue and white logo on it and twirled it between her fingers. She smiled, her eyes widening in bewilderment.

"You earned it."

Dani leapt from her bed and hugged her father.

"Thank you, Daddy."

"You're very welcome. Just remember, you earned it."

"Coolest father *ever!*" Dani returned to her bed, a huge grin on her face.

"Don't be up too late." Dennis turned away and left the room. Dani watched him go, biting her lip in excitement. After a second, she climbed back on the bed and returned to her work. She glanced at her clock. It was a little before midnight. She checked her phone.

Still no text from Ben.

*Arsehole*. She placed the BMW key beside her phone.

"One more hour."

Dani resumed typing.

# FOUR

Ross Rhodes sat at his expensive oak desk, his feet up and crossed, watching the wall mounted TV that sat above his grand fireplace. The remote was in his hand, aimed in no particular direction. His dark eyes were on the headline that was flashing across the bottom of the screen.

*BREAKING: Multiple gunshot victim survives assault.*

According to the graphics, a plucky, redheaded reporter, with too much Botox and not enough cleavage, was interviewing a Detective Inspector Scott. Her forehead was enormous and her technique brash and naïve. The DI was revealing minimal details about the crime. All he knew was that the victim, a talented Italian chef from Soho, survived a shooting attempt, leaving him paralysed, but alive. He also suffered traumatic injuries to his face and body. A huge amount of rehab was expected and no further details were available. After a moment, he sidled away as the reporter turned to the viewers and signed off.

Rhodes turned off the TV with a click on the remote.

As if on cue, Bradley, his right hand man, entered the large office. The former boxer, with bulging muscles squeezed into a six-foot-three frame, was all controlled rage and confidence. His suit was tight with a daily gym routine and a balanced diet.

His hair was clipped short, his face chiseled in all the wrong places, giving him an air of menace. He stood silently at Rhodes' desk, awaiting instruction.

Rhodes tossed the remote across the room and it hit the wall with a thud. He glanced up at Bradley, who didn't move. Rhodes laughed. "You know, Bradley, I saw this day coming. I should have gone with my gut and done it myself."

"How shall I proceed, sir?" Bradley asked, his grizzly voice belying a degree in sports science and an IQ of one hundred and forty six. His chiseled arms crossed against his barreled chest.

"Kill the chef. I'll teach him to cut me out of any protection. Cunt. He'll be in hospital somewhere, probably St Barts. Get Sanchez on it, he can blend in and become a doctor for a few hours. In and out, keep it quiet."

Bradley blinked, as if capturing the instruction for later. "Anything else?"

"Yeah, kill the shooter. I don't accept liabilities."

"Dennis?"

"Yeah, he couldn't even kill a fucking chef. What sort of reputation does that give my organisation? Kill him, him and his fucking family."

*****

The southern rectory provided Dani with a relaxing shortcut, a quicker way to make it home. In bad weather, or if she wanted to avoid someone in particular, she preferred the isolated trip it guaranteed her. The path was nothing more than a dirt track covered in mulch, shrouded by elegant, whispering trees, and flanked by manicured lawns and expertly shaped foliage. However, it provided more peace and quiet than the winding roads that cut between multiple businesses, abrupt concrete behemoths and noisy homes.

More importantly, it kept her away from other people.

Despite her class potential as a nerd, Dani didn't fit into any cliques at school. Bullies didn't gravitate towards her, but nerds didn't see her as one of their own either. In reality, people didn't bother her. This continued into college and she was thankful for it. Blending in made life simpler and less of a distraction. She liked her alone time.

Teddy was staying behind for football tonight and would be an hour or two behind her. She knew her mother was collecting him anyway, so it gave her the chance to walk out of college, fast, and head straight home. Alone.

Avoiding people wasn't an issue. Until today.

Right now, she was avoiding one person.

Ben.

*Avoiding might be a strong word. You're pissed at him is all.*

Dani sighed, head down. Her footsteps gathered pace.

She hadn't received a text or call from him in three days. Whether his phone was charged or not, three days was no excuse. She couldn't remember the last time someone her age hadn't worshipped a mobile phone.

Nowadays, a mobile phone was a teenager's sole method of existence in the palm of their work-shy hands. They did everything through it. It irked Dani a little; herself brought up differently, to respect people somewhat, she preferred an actual conversation, human interaction. Most of her friends – the few she could actually class as such – lived by the mobile. Conversations took place via shortened, grammar offending text messages or visual telephone calls. Once, she'd seen two girls 'face timing' one another from across the room, when it would have been simpler, and cheaper, to stand up, walk three feet and say hello. Conversation of the most basic kind seemed lost on youth today. Technology really was eroding the cerebral potential to evolve.

She was looking forward to finishing her book when she got in. The mobile phone would be the least of her concerns this evening. Dani gazed up, looking through the trees, and realised dark clouds had formed overhead.

A chilled wind rippled her trouser legs. The first droplet of rain exploded on her cold cheek. She hiked up her collar and turned the corner, into the rectory. Four minutes more, and she'd emerge by Kambo's and seconds later, cross the road to home.

*Not long now.*

Her eyes levelled and she stopped in her tracks. Squinting, she observed the park before her. The lush green grass wavered in the ever-increasing wind. Beyond the greenery, several trees swayed, their leaves taking flight and curling to the ground slowly. Three houses stood idle, one inhabitant standing on his front porch, sipping from a beer can. His white fence, the only house to possess one, was creaking and wobbling before him. He glanced at it with disdain and vanished into his abode. Several kids rode by on bikes, their faces heading into the biting wind.

Dani took a step back.

Her eyes weren't on the houses, or nature's contribution to the rectory, or even the reckless kids speeding towards an open public road that ran parallel to the rectory itself. Her eyes were on the bench beneath the trees, a black, iron monstrosity built in honor of some old person who'd helped the community for several decades.

On the bench sat Ben.

He wasn't alone.

Dani looked for something to hide behind. She was standing on the longest pavement in the rectory; its exclusive surrounding was the kept grass. She reckoned diving to the ground might attract some attention.

Instead, she just stood there. Ben didn't see her, he wasn't even aware of his surroundings; much less his girlfriend who'd stumbled on his deceitful secret. His lips were too busy kissing the blonde woman perched on the bench beside him.

Every few seconds or so, he would come up for air, stroke her cheek or push her wind ruffled hair aside. She smiled, lost in the moment. They were simply two teenagers in love.

That's how Dani realised this wasn't just a fling.

The body language spoke of a familiar relationship, comfort born from a long-term coupling. Comfort born from a sexual relationship. There was no sexual edge, no petting above the clothing, no urge to take the woman to his house for a quick fuck. He was simply enjoying the public display of affection for what it was – a stopgap until the next time they had sex.

Dani felt the sting of tears behind her eyes. Instantly, she rubbed them, refusing to shed a tear for this bastard. The quick movement of her hand caught the blond haired girl's attention. She glanced at Dani, her eyes looking through her, recognition not imminent. Within seconds, Ben noticed and followed her gaze. The smile dropped from his face.

*No time like the present,* she thought.

Her father's voice echoed in her mind. *Men are a distraction. You have to go through a lot of shit before you find a diamond. You're too young to know what love is.*

As she stepped forward, she nodded, agreeing with her father for the very first time. His wisdom had seemed like social venom in the past. She didn't let on about her true feelings. Now? From this moment forward, her father was the most sensible man on the planet.

Her eyes were on the path that led out of the rectory. She was minutes from her home. Instead of following it, she ambled right and arrived before the young couple, on instinct, as if guided on autopilot. Dani had to settle this. The blonde girl smiled. "Can I help you?"

"Hello…I don't know…Ben?"

Ben shuffled uncomfortably. He sheepishly looked at his companion and stood up. "Hi, Dani."

Dani said nothing, her vehement glare speaking volumes.

"Ben, who is this?" The blonde girl stood up beside him, clutching his arm.

"I'm his girlfriend," Dani blurted.

The smile disappeared from the blonde-haired woman's face.

She released his arm, backing away. "Noooo, *I'm* his girlfriend." On that note, both women stared at Ben.

"I can explain." Ben looked from one woman to the other. "I can explain…"

"You have thirty seconds," Dani said, her voice controlled. Her stomach was doing backflips, and she was on the verge of vomiting, but she retained control. Her father had taught her better.

"Dani, this is Chantelle. Chantelle…Dani."

They nodded at one another.

"Dani…Chantelle has been my girlfriend for six months."

"You've been dating me for three," she replied.

Chantelle gasped, her hands shooting to her mouth. Within seconds, she buckled and sat on the iron bench, nearly missing the seat edge. Dani looked at her and felt a shot of regret, a shred of pity. She thought it funny, considering her own emotions were on the verge of pushing her to a breakdown.

Ben sat beside her. "I'm sorry, Chantelle. I never aimed for you to find out this way.

Chantelle nodded, her jaw jostling in anger. She stood up on wobbly legs. Ben reached out for her and placed his hands on her arms. "You're the one I love…"

"Is that because she lets you *fuck* her?"

Ben and Chantelle both glared at Dani. Dani, her eyes still stinging from the prickle of tears, crossed her arms. "Well, was it?"

Chantelle narrowed her eyes. "Wait, you *didn't* fuck her?"

Ben looked from Dani to Chantelle and shook his head quickly. "No, no, I didn't. She meant nothing. She's frigid as hell."

A solitary tear slid down Dani's face. The taste of vomit was rising in her throat. A burning anger was slithering through Dani's veins. *Leave now,* she thought. *It can only get worse.*

"If you didn't fuck her, that's not cheating."

Ben did a second take. "What, wait…huh?"

"You only kissed her? That's nothing. Kissing don't count. You didn't stick your dick in her, that's fine. You're forgiven."

Ben's face lit up.

He stepped closer to Chantelle. Dani shook her head. Chantelle smiled, licked her lips and looked at the dejected woman. "You hear that, skank? He chose me. He didn't even stick his cock in you, which says it all. You can leave now."

Ben nodded. "I think that's best, don't you, Dani?" He was unsuccessfully attempting to hide a smug smile.

Dani, her soul shattered, her veins on fire and fists clenched, turned and walked out of the rectory. As she went, she shouted back. "You deserve each other."

Ben and Chantelle didn't give her another look.

Dani rounded the fence at the entrance and walked into the street. Placing her hand on a lamppost, she breathed out heavily and wretched. Vomit splattered the pavement at her feet. No one stopped to assist her. After a moment, she stood up and wiped her mouth.

The short walk to her house was a blur. The street, vehicles, and people before her passed in slow motion, their faces nondescript, their noises indecipherable in her emotionally shredded brain. Her vision wobbled from side to side. People laughed and pointed, probably at the acidic mess on her chin, but she paid it no heed. After what seemed like an hour, she arrived outside Kambo's. The smell of confectionary brought on an instant wave of nausea and she vomited again, this time splattering her shoes.

*Why, Ben? Why did you do this to me?*

She remembered Ben leaving her yesterday, heading back the very way she'd just stumbled. She'd been blissfully unaware, delightfully happy. Her mind started to piece together the untruthful pieces of his dark deceit.

*When did it start?*

*How many times?*

*Did he kiss her before kissing you?*

*Did he go down on...*

Dani closed her eyes and shook the thought away. Wiping her eyes, she crossed the road, holding out a hand in case a car was nearby and her vision prevented her from seeing it.

She reached her front door, pushed it open, and wobbled up the stairs.

She kicked off her vomit soaked shoes and tossed her bag and coat on the floor. Dani staggered to her bed, lifting her vomit-caked sweater over her head, and fell forward, rolling as she did, landing sideways. The plush duvet swallowed her broken body. Dani wrapped it around her, seeking its protection. Only when she laid her head on her pillow did she let out the emotion.

Dani screamed into the pillow. Then, the tears came. The floodgates opened.

Teddy walked past the door, saw his sister, and stopped. He remained silent.

# FIVE

Sanchez slipped a stick of raspberry gum into his mouth and began to chew slowly.

His steely blue eyes, concealed behind a pair of dark shades, darted back and forth, watching the entrance to St. Barts, the local general hospital. Despite the biting winds and the drizzle in the damp air, he stood alert, rooted to the corner of the street by an empty, graffiti-decorated bus stop. The battered brown coat that kept him warm, coupled with his disheveled look, gave him the appearance of a typical Londoner, a person no different to the next seventy people who walked across the average line of sight.

Blending in.

Sanchez did it better than anyone.

Observation was boring and conclusive. In thirty minutes, he'd seen six nurses, seven doctors, more than a dozen patients, two pizza deliveries, and a hobbling, drunk clown.

But not one security guard.

Sanchez wasn't convinced, knowing that the wannabe police officers probably made a beeline for the break room for coffee and potential doughnuts rather than fresh air and social interactions with smokers and bored taxi drivers. As his gaze returned to the entrance, he saw one such driver flip off a patient in a pink dressing gown and drive away.

That rage, coupled with the dark blood splashed across her shoulder, and her distracted state, indicated a head wound, a loss of equilibrium and lack of a tip, a tip that would have paid for the cleaning of any spilt bodily fluids from her journey.

Sanchez shook his head, a minimal movement that meant nothing in a social setting. Maybe he was frustrated at the weather. On the other hand, the bus being late – or absent as the case may be, none had driven by in the past hour – was enough to make the average person shake his head. Sanchez imagined the normal people concerning themselves with such rigmarole, such uselessness.

He positioned the gum on his tongue, flattened it against the roof of his mouth and sighed deeply. After a moment, he stepped onto the road that arched down to the entrance of St. Barts. The drizzle spattered across his glasses, blurring his view. In one swift movement, he swiped them from his face and pocketed them, his eyes ever alert. His footsteps clonked loudly on the concrete causeway, one vacated by ambulances and other vehicles.

He stepped under the glass awning, ignoring the charity collector who shook a jingly plastic pot at him, and walked into the hospital.

The smell of disinfectant and cleanliness hit him immediately, but he didn't stop. He strolled past the reception desk, a mask of indifference and false, muted pain on his face, and walked to the lifts.

No one watched him, no one cared.

A child tossed a Frisbee across the waiting room, the object clonked loudly on some glass, startling some of the sick patients. Yes, no one noticed him; people had more pressing matters to concern themselves with.

Sanchez pushed the button for floor 4 and stood back, leaning on the wall. He watched as a man in a leg cast hobbled across the waiting room to a chair, fresh from a visit to the toilet. A woman with a thick bandage wrapped around her head was crying into the shoulder of a loved one, a doting, blonde-haired man with bad acne and skinny jeans.

The kid with the Frisbee began to cry as his parents admonished him for his stupidity.

The lifts opened, empty, but Sanchez didn't move. He checked his watch and nodded.

The doors closed again.

The reception nurse had her head down, her worries and gaze buried in a mass of paperwork, work that would never be complete. Her frizzled, curly hair and creased forehead spoke of stress and job fatigue. Her colleague, a fresh-faced redhead with adorable freckles and an innocent smile powered by natural energy, one yet to be exhausted and destroyed by her chosen profession, bounced around behind her. Sanchez could practically see the vehemence rising from the older nurse.

Sanchez noticed movement in his peripheral vision and saw an elderly woman move for the elevators. He pushed the button for floor 4 again, receiving a wary glance and a half-smile from the woman. He nodded, turning away.

He checked his watch.

The lift dinged and he stepped into it. The old woman didn't follow, holding back, refusing to share a lift with the strange man. The disgusting look she gave him was unmistakable, one of old-school philosophy and belief.

*Fucking spik.*

Sanchez could imagine the words seething from her shortsighted, racist eyes. She probably thought he was going to mug her or attempt to sell her a burrito. The lift doors closed, erasing the woman from sight. The car shunted as it started its ascent.

After a moment, the car eased to a halt. The doors slid apart and Sanchez stepped out onto the fourth floor.

The hallway, one deprived of a reception desk and waiting room, was silent, the minimal bustle of hospital staff merely a background noise.

Again, he stepped to the wall opposite and waited once more.

He checked his watch. After a minute, a hospital cleaner rolled a cart around the corner and headed his way.

*Right on time.*

He pushed the button for floor 5.

Sanchez rolled the gum on his tongue and, lifting a hand to his lips, spat it into his palm. The man walked to a bin, lifted the lid and emptied it into a swelling, transparent trash bag. As he did, Sanchez dropped the gum onto the floor, in line with the trash cart.

Sanchez backed away, giving the man room to pass, who nodded at him, thanking him silently. He rolled the cart past the elevators, the wheels missing the gum. However, his shoe caught it and stamped it flat, pushing it into the grip of his sole.

After a few hindered steps, the man stopped and hoisted his shoe in the air, looking for the cause of his sticky walk. "For fuck's sake," he cursed under his breath, the words carrying on the near-silence. He bent down and untied his shoelace, plucked the shoe off his foot and rooted in his cart for a suitable tool to remove the gum.

Sanchez stepped forward; the man's back turned, lifting the bunch of keys from his belt buckle and pocketing them in one movement. Three seconds later, the lift doors slid aside. Sanchez stepped into the car and waited. The doors closed and the car, once again, shot up.

He was on the fifth floor within seconds.

Sanchez exited the lift and turned left. Glancing left and right, the hall was empty bar one police officer. He reclined on a metal chair reading a magazine. As expected, he was guarding the chef following the previous murder attempt.

*Nice and simple*, thought Sanchez.

He took a USB stick from his jeans and placed it against the keys in his pocket. It buzzed twice in his hand. Separating the two, he walked past the sentry slowly and paused, stopping at a vending machine several feet down the hall.

The chef's door was wide open, closer to him than the police officer.

Aside from the sentry, the hallway was deserted.

*Quiet day.* Sanchez smiled.

The timing was everything.

He thumbed two coins into the machine and pushed the same button twice. Two cans of Sprite dropped into the chute. Collecting them, he walked back the way he came and stopped before the officer, who looked up. Sanchez saw his shoulders tense. "Can I help you, sir?"

"Sure. I just bought a drink from the machine and it gave me two. I wondered if you fancied it. Since you're doing your civil duty and all. We all hate hospitals."

The officer narrowed his eyes and smiled. "Sure thing, thanks. Much appreciated."

"No problem." Sanchez nodded and began to walk away. The officer followed him, several steps behind, as expected.

*Perfect.*

Sanchez walked into the next room. The officer strolled by, oblivious, and Sanchez stepped back into the hallway silently. The officer rounded a corner, disappearing, vacating his duties for a moment.

Sanchez walked back towards the chef's unguarded domain and stopped, tossing the keys into the room. The magnetized bunch of metal skated on the tiled floor and landed next to the electrical machines that rose and streamed above the bed. Within seconds, the machines started to buzz and whine, the strong magnets going to work on the complicated waves and technology within.

Sanchez looked down the hallway.

Still quiet.

He pulled a silenced Sig Sauer P228 from his coat and fired twice, hitting the chef in the head both times, a quick double tap.

Blood spattered his pillow and blanket, the unconscious man thrashed in the bed, the bullets thrashing him like an electrical current. He died instantly, the silenced *whups* buried beneath a racket of noisy machinery. A flat line indicated his demise, but was soon lost beneath a cacophony of buzzing and beeps.

Sanchez walked back to the other room and stepped in, holstering his weapon, just as the police officer returned with several nurses, all rushing to the chef's aid.

They passed him without a thought.

Sanchez looked at the comatose old lady in the bed before him, stroked her wrinkled face, and smiled.

He stepped out of the room and disappeared, the noise and chaos around him providing the perfect cover. No one saw him leave.

*****

"Dennis, I'm going to order pizza. What do you want?"

"Plain for me." Dennis was sitting in his armchair, reading the new Stephen King book, immersed, and not even looking up.

Carla nodded and turned to Teddy. "What do you want?"

"Ham and pineapple?"

"Okay…gross, but okay." Carla walked to the foot of the stairs and shouted. "Dani?"

A muffled voice answered. "What?"

"I'm ordering pizza. What do you want?"

"I'm not hungry…"

"You will be though, what do you want?"

A pause. Carla heard her daughter sigh before responding. "Pepperoni, please."

"Good." Carla dialed the pizzeria number into her phone and ordered the food with a side of wedges, nachos and garlic bread. After a moment, she hung up and slumped onto the sofa.

"Dani is really going for it with her course. Never thought I would see a kid work so hard." Carla smiled.

"She's a right boffin," said Teddy. He was doing a puzzle on the carpet, confused by the fact it was two sided. The same image on both sides made it extremely difficult. His tongue was protruding from his mouth, firm with concentration. He currently had the edges pieced together and was now working on the centre. Carla frowned. "That's not a nice thing to say about your sister."

"So? She calls me douceface all the time."

"No she doesn't," said Carla, lying. Dennis laughed in the background, exposing his wife's lie. Carla groaned. "Well, it's still not nice."

Teddy placed a piece in the jigsaw and punched the air in celebration. He scooped another handful from the box and placed them on the carpet. "I saw Dani cry today."

Carla and Dennis both looked at their son. Dennis flicked his eyes towards Carla and nodded, his eyes speaking clearly. *This sounds like a girl problem.* Carla nodded. "When, honey?"

"When I got back from football. We couldn't play because of the rain so I came home early. I went to my room, that's when I saw her." Carla nodded and stood up, preparing to pay her daughter a visit. Dennis looked over. "Leave her be. She likes being alone, you know that."

"Why would she cry?"

"Who knows? She's a teenager," he replied.

"She's a strong teenager, not like many I know. It must be serious."

"She'll be fine. If it's boy troubles, all kids need it. It makes them sensible."

"Parent of the Year over here," Carla smiled. "I suppose you're…oh, hang on."

Muted footsteps sounded on the hallway floor above and Dani emerged on the stairs. She stopped halfway down, leaning on the wooden bannister. "Mum, what weekend are we going away again?"

"The 16th. Why?" Carla looked at Dani. The tear streaks were all but gone, darkening her normally vibrant eyes. The normal electricity in those brown orbs was vacant.

"I have a field trip, and I really want to go. I think it's the week after, so cool."

"How much is it?"

"Thirty pounds, that okay?"

"I'm sure we can stretch the purse strings a little." Carla smiled.

"Thanks, Mum." Dani drummed her fingers on the bannister.

Carla frowned. "You okay, honey?"

"Yeah…yeah, nothing I can't handle."

"Okay. If you need a chat…"

"Yeah, yeah. I know. Thanks though, for the trip. I'm looking forward to it."

The doorbell rang. Carla stood up and checked her watch. "My, that was quick." She ambled over to the door. Teddy ran over to the stairs and started to harass his sister. "Hey, it's dobber boffin face."

"Seriously? Go away, *squirt.*"

"*Never*, I'm here to harass you until…"

*BLAM.*

Carla's shredded body flew across the living room and smashed into the TV, knocking it to the ground with a huge crash. The attached cables wrenched boxes and units from the shelf above, sending them toppling to the wooden floor. One bounced off the dying woman's face with a violent clonk. Blood sprayed and sluiced in all directions from a multitude of ragged holes in her tattered torso. Blood frothed from her mouth and a loud gargle signaled her final throe.

Dennis stood up, dropping his book. Dani and Teddy turned their heads to the chaos in horror. Dani stepped to the bottom of the stairs, pulling her brother behind her.

Dennis looked at his kids. "Get Teddy out of here."

A huge man stepped through the front door. He was dressed entirely in black, from his suit, to his balaclava and gloves. Even the shotgun in his hands was gleaming and charcoal coloured. He looked like a modernized version of Death, his scythe replaced by a pump action shotgun. His boots crunched on the shattered glass, signaling his arrival.

He turned to Teddy and Dani and lifted the gun.

Dennis ran over from the left and swung a fist. His punch smacked the intruder in the face. The giant move sideways, dropping the gun. Dennis, realising time was tight, turned to his children once more. "Get out! Go! *Take the car and run!*"

Dennis turned back to the man before him. He buckled as the man crashed a giant fist into his ribs, and head-butted him, shattering three teeth and slicing his tongue. His gum ripped, filling his mouth with warm blood. Dennis fell backwards, crimson spooling from his damaged mouth. He looked at Dani, pleading, gurgling. "Go…"

Dani pushed Teddy up the stairs, propelled by absolute fear. "Teddy, go. My room, now."

"What about the car?"

"Not now, *go*!"

"Upstairs is stupid; I've seen enough movies to know that!"

She realised it *was* a stupid move, but she needed to get the key and she wasn't about to leave her brother alone. Between a rock and a black-clad psychopath. "*Just fucking go.*"

Teddy sprinted up the stairs, stumbling on the top stair as it appeared too quickly for his small feet. He rounded the hallway and ran above Dani's head. Dani followed slowly, keeping an eye on her father. He was fighting off the intruder. Torn between saving her father and her brother, Dani groaned and climbed the stairs.

Teddy was standing in his doorway.

"Dani, quick, in here." Dani ran towards him, her eyes wide. She motioned to her brother. "We should go to my room; we can climb out of the window. It's next to the garage."

Teddy looked past her, watching the stairs with serious concern. "Or, we can hide in my den. He'll never find us in there."

Dani stopped, saying nothing. After a second, she realised it was a brilliant idea. She needed to do one thing first. She held up a finger, indicating for her brother to wait a second, and ran into her room. With a shuffle of the wrist, she unlatched her window and pushed it wide open, into the cool, evening air. She knocked a few books to the floor, making it look like they'd escaped through the window. She hurried back to the hallway and watched the stairs.

A gunshot rang out, crippling her confidence. It was followed by a loud thump as something heavy hit the wooden floor.

*Dad?*

Then, the footsteps came. Loud, methodical.

Not her fathers, he was barefoot. These were leather boots, heavy and solid.

Edging towards the stairs.

*Shit.*

Using every inch of will power, and ignoring the warm tears streaming down her face, Dani ambled to Teddy's room and shoved him through the door. She closed it, holding the handle down to make sure it did so silently, and turned to her brother. He was already rifling through his wardrobe, clearing aside a skateboard and some clothes. Within seconds he slid a panel sideways, Dani watched it disappear behind his hanging shirts and trousers.

The entrance was half a door's height, a practical cubbyhole. Teddy ducked down and entered, sliding into the crevice with expertise. Dani walked quickly to it, dropped to her knees and closed the wardrobe behind her. She then crawled into the space and slid the panel shut.

The space was the size of a small, slim room, tucked between two walls – between their bedrooms. For a small boy, it was huge.

Darkness enveloped everything, but she could make out posters, toys and some comics strewn to the side. An unused torch sat beside them, propped on a pile of batteries. Dani noticed the opposite side of the wall and realised her wardrobe was beyond it. She shuffled closer, putting her ear to the surface, listening for the intruder.

She heard nothing.

She leaned back against the wooden beams and wiped her face. Instinctively, she reached for her brother's hand and held it tight. It was cold and clammy, shaking. She could feel his small frame trembling next to her. She pulled him in close, warming him with a sisterly hug. Slowly, her shirt started to dampen under his tears. They were streaming down his face. He didn't say a word.

For a long moment, they sat in silence.

Then they heard the footsteps.

They were nothing more than muted thuds on carpet. They came from Dani's room. She envisioned the huge man stalking across her bedroom, seeing the window, thinking they'd escaped, and leaving. She wanted the ordeal to end. For a moment, a long, hope tinged moment; she thought he'd done just that.

When her wardrobe doors flung open, smashing against the drawers on the other side of the wall with a loud wooden clunk, she flinched. Teddy held her tighter. She placed a hand over his mouth tightly, keeping him quiet. The clattering of coat hangers smashing against one another, and soft, muted clumps as clothing hit the bottom of the wardrobe, was all they could hear. Dani wanted to close her eyes but found her brain wouldn't let her. She expected the panel by her side to slide by any second. To see the balaclava face poke through and smile, before a meaty hand reached in and grabbed them.

It didn't.

It wouldn't happen. Her shoe rack was right in front of the panel, nestled at the back of her wardrobe. Besides, from her side of the hidden alcove, it didn't open anyway. Dad had wallpapered over it.

*Dad.* A feeling of huge loss nearly overwhelmed her.

Dani realised she was holding her breath. Turning her head to Teddy, she gazed at her brother. She could see the top of his head; it was shaking, trembling with absolute fear. His brown, tousled hair flinched with every movement. She felt terrible. After a moment, Dani focused on the sounds again. She realised they'd stopped.

*Was he standing on the other side? Listening?*

Dani felt a squirming, harrowing dread in the pit of her stomach. She crossed her legs, hoping she wouldn't pee in front of her brother.

Then the footsteps left. They grew fainter as he walked away.

Dani finally breathed out. The air whistled through her nostrils and she realised they were clogged with snot. She wiped her face but didn't dare sniff. Any slight sound right now would be lethal.

She waited five minutes, checking her watch constantly. Her brother didn't change position or stop trembling. The tears had subdued though.

It was now or never.

She moved Teddy away from her chest. "Teddy," she whispered.

Her brother glanced up at her, his eyes ringed with red raw skin, puffy from rivulets of horror-induced tears. He nodded, not saying anything.

"We need to make a run for it, okay?"

Teddy shook his head and instantly hugged back into her chest again. Dani patted him on the back and allowed it to happen for a moment. She pulled him away again. "I need you to be brave, okay?"

Teddy shook his head, his bottom lip quivering. He sniffed silently, his face screwed in an expression of absolute loss and terror. Dani felt her guts lurch.

*What am I doing? He just saw his mother murdered. We should stay here; he's in no shape to move.*

*He'll find us.*

*He hasn't so far.*

*It's only a matter of time.*

*We can't stay here. We need to go.*

*Where are the police?*

Dani knew she had no choice. If they stayed here, they wouldn't last the night. The police would come, maybe, after the gunshots. It could take them all night though.

They needed to get out now.

She counted to three in her head. She pulled Teddy away. "Right, we need to go out through your room, down the hall and into my room, okay? We can climb out onto the roof and get into the garage. I can grab my mobile phone too and we can call the police. Then, we'll be safe, okay?"

"What about Mom and Dad?"

The question slammed her in the ribs, knocking the breath out of her. She felt a warm sensation of nausea crawling through her blood. She gulped, realising she couldn't chicken out now. Their lives depended on it. Vomiting wouldn't help anyone in this confined space and it would alert the intruder.

Wherever he was.

"We'll help Mom and Dad when we're out. We need to get away from the killer first, okay?" Dani felt like she was deserting her parents. She wondered what Dad would do in this situation. If they were…dead…going back for them would get her and her brother killed. It was a harsh decision, but a sensible one.

Teddy nodded. He wiped his face with his sleeve.

"On three. One, two…" Dani gulped. "Three."

Teddy slid the panel aside and silently crawled into the wardrobe. Dani followed him. Her brother stood up and cautiously opened the wardrobe door.

After a second, he pushed the door wide. He turned back to Dani and smiled.

"The coast is clea…"

Teddy's head exploded, showering Dani with brains and skull and blood.

Dani screamed.

# SIX

The mission was going according to plan.

Bradley had taken it upon himself to carry out Rhodes' demand. After the fuck up that Dennis made, he didn't want his boss disappointed again. No repeats and no failures. Rhodes was much easier to work for when he got what he wanted.

Bradley aimed to give him that.

He lowered the shotgun and watched the dead boy topple back into the wardrobe. A grin spread over his lips. He felt the balaclava tickle his facial muscles as he did so. He rolled his tongue over his teeth, dislodging one that Dennis had loosened with his fist. Blood started seeping into his mouth and Bradley rolled the tooth around his bloody tongue before swallowing it, without flinching.

He stood and waited.

He knew the kids were in the partition between the wardrobes. Rhodes had provided a blueprint of the house, as expected. His boss could get anything at a moment's notice and it helped him to be prepared. The girl would listen to her younger brother because, as circumstances dictated, she'd needed to keep him safe. No kid was going to ignore a hideaway hole that no one knew about...well, almost no one.

He instantly knew this is where the kids would head.

They'd ignored their father's instruction – as most kids normally do, it must be in their genes or something – before he'd put a bullet between Dennis's eyes. He had fight in him, he'd not expected that. I suppose anyone would if their kids were threatened and their wife was dead inches from them. He'd kicked the body over after shooting him. Taking one last look around the room, he'd ambled upstairs.

The look of Dennis' life ebbing away had made Bradley hard. He got a thrill out of killing people. Carla was a treat. For a split second, he'd been able to ogle her fantastic tits in her tight jumper, those curvy legs swathed in denim. He imagined burying his mouth between her shapely legs, sniffing and lapping at her sex, and bringing her to a violent orgasm. Except, instead of ejaculate, it would be blood seeping from between her legs as he tore her clitoris from her body, chewed it like a sliver of beef and swallowed. He'd then fuck the bloody hole until he released inside of her.

Instead, he shot her. He'd never seen a woman fly so far.

When he saw the daughter, things got interesting.

He couldn't have her, he knew that, but that didn't mean he couldn't take the body with him. For a few days, the body would be fun. He could spend some quality time with her before it decomposed. Hell, maybe he could take Carla too and have a naughty threesome.

Bradley groaned as his penis throbbed in his pants.

*You have a job to do…*

The image of a mutilated Carla had allowed him to stride into the household, full of confidence and with a raging boner.

A boner that promised to remain for an hour at least.

He snapped back to the mission. The girl, buried somewhere in the closet, screamed.

"I know you're there," Bradley hissed. Silence greeted him. His voice was raspy; his lungs were pumping air and shortening his breath. "You can't escape."

Still no sound. He imagined the girl hiding behind the closed door, staring at her dead brother, maybe going insane.

He imagined her eyes wide, her lips trembling.

*Do nipples get hard when you're scared?*

*I've never had my dick sucked by an insane girl before...especially not a prize like her.*

Bradley closed his eyes and cursed silently. *You have a job to do.*

A *snick snack* shattered the silence as he reloaded the shotgun. *Let's finish this.*

# SEVEN

The feeling was alien to Dani.

New.

Unfamiliar. She'd never felt it before.

As she stared at her dead brother's corpse, his eviscerated skull nothing but a bloody stump on the top of his neck, she felt her body stiffening, her brain shutting down. No, not shutting down, adapting, and shutting *out* the horror before her.

Protecting her.

The inside of the wardrobe was illuminated by Teddy's nightlight, its sole purpose to circle on the spot beside his bed, filling the room with comforting light, to keep the monster in the wardrobe away.

Except today, a sickening role-reversal was occurring; the monster was on the outside of the wardrobe and the innocent inside.

It wasn't comforting in the slightest.

Dani watched her brother's sticky cerebral tissue slowly slide down the wardrobe's interior wall, propelled by splattered blood and shattered bone fragments. Occasionally, a star or a circle, cast in light, would dance over the massacre innocently, as if nothing had happened. A chunk of brain slipped to the ground, colliding with one of the skateboard wheels, spinning it with a low creak.

Dani's eyes flicked around the small, dark space and she realised the feeling of terror was subsiding and being replaced by something else, something...new.

She glanced down and saw her brother's blood, spattered all over her shirt and jeans. Her hands moved automatically to it and pulled away dark, glistening red, trembling. Her warm, wet eyes closed for a moment, urging herself not to lose it.

"I know you're in there."

The hissing voice, muffled by fabric and laboured breathing, was confronting her. It was the first time she'd heard him speak. Dani opened her eyes and realised she had little choice here, trapped in a wardrobe, between an impassable wall and a man with a shotgun. She swallowed, her dry, scratchy throat making it significantly more difficult. Dani ran ideas through her head and everything came back to one answer.

Surrender.

She couldn't give up; the intruder massacred her family, right before her eyes. *I'm a dead woman if I give up.*

"You can't escape."

And there it was.

The truth.

Dani knew this was game over. There was no other choice. She closed her eyes and let the tears roll. She slumped to the ground, landing on Teddy's soft toys – the ones he denied having because he was a 'big boy now' – and resigned.

Guilt wracked her body, making her shake. The tears rolled off her face, dripping onto her blood-soaked shirt, trickling down her chin and onto her neck, making it damp. She felt like she was deserting her family.

The footsteps approached, slowly, muffled on the blue carpet that Teddy had chosen himself. Any second now, the man would aim the shotgun at her face and end her life. Dani didn't move, didn't change position, and didn't look up.

She awaited her fate.

*You'll be seeing Teddy, Mom and Dad very soon.*

A giant hand reached into the wardrobe and grasped Dani by the hair. She screamed, kicking and thrashing as she did so, before the intruder yanked her into the room. Her feet dragged through the gory remains of her brother, soaking her socks with blood and cerebral tissue. Within seconds, she found herself thrown to the carpet. Her elbows skidded on the rough surface, chafing the soft skin. During the fall, she bit her lip, drawing blood. She composed herself and turned her back to the window, facing her attacker. Her sore eyes looked up at the black behemoth before her. Her lip throbbed.

"Finally, we meet. Hello, Danielle."

Dani wiped her face with her sleeve. She spat blood onto the carpet. "Fuck you."

"Now, now. That's no way to greet the guest of the house. Your mother would be ashamed of you if she heard that. Not that she can."

Dani licked the crimson from her lips. "Don't you talk about my…"

The behemoth lunged forward and kicked Dani in the face. Her head snapped back, pain surged to her brain and she groaned, collapsing face first to the carpet. Agony coursed through her tiny body. "I'll talk about anything I want to, young lady. You can't stop me."

Dani pushed herself onto her blood-soaked hands and crawled away, her head pounding with vehement torment. Holding her weight, her arms wobbled, threatening to collapse at any second. She kept one blurry eye on her attacker. He stepped sideways, following his foe.

"Now, let's talk about you."

Dani said nothing. Her eyes didn't leave the intruder.

"When I came home tonight…I saw your mother. My, what a piece. In a different life, in a different profession, I could have had the time of my life with your mother. Your father wouldn't have stopped me; hell, I would have made him watch as I made her squeal. Things changed though, when I saw you."

Dani clenched with fear, a swelling emerged in her stomach. She remembered a chat with her mother once. What did she say? *Men are only after one thing. Consent is everything. If you're not ready, don't feel forced into it.*

Her mind flashed back to Ben. Ben kissing Chantelle.

*Was that the reason? She wanted to wait and he couldn't – wouldn't?*

*You're thinking about this now?*

Dani snapped back to reality. She positioned herself on her knees, ready to fight should the behemoth lay a hand on her.

"Things changed. I took one look at you…that fine arse, those shoulders; your skin colour is divine. Even your tits have come in nicely, which is no surprise having seen your mother. And, as much as I would take my sweet time, scour every inch of your body with my tongue and probe every wet crevice gently, then roughly, I can't do that. You're only seventeen. I may be a monster, I admit that, but I have my limits. We built our organisation on respect, loyalty and integrity. If it had been a few years later, when you were twenty, then I would wreck you. But, alas, that isn't to be." The attacker lowered his shotgun and placed it against the wall.

Dani climbed to her feet. Her eyes flicked to the door, her escape. Dani wondered if she could run to the car and get out before this hulking slab of muscle caught her. Her hand patted her thigh, feeling the car key there, her salvation.

She was confident she could do it.

She didn't have a chance.

The behemoth ducked and thrust a hand up towards her throat. Dani's lithe body elevated from the carpet, propelled through the air, and crashed against the wall. Her rump came to a rest on top of a chest of drawers, which now sat below her. She choked, slapping at the hand that was pinning her to the wall by her throat, killing her. The grip loosened, and Dani could breathe again. Her eyes stared at the attacker, his eyes hidden behind an unnecessary pair of sunglasses. For the first time, she realised every inch of him was covered in black.

His head cocked to the side, as if observing her. Like prey.

*Smart*, she thought. *No DNA traces.*

Her heart sunk, realising no one would solve the murders.

She had to stay alive.

"Danielle, you're way too young for me. However, I feel I'm missing something glorious here. I don't see many women of your calibre in my job, well, women with dignity. I see whores and hookers every day. I mean, who would stick their cock in one of those? Why do that when you can have a glorious, tight virgin, like yourself?"

Dani said nothing. She simply stared at the man. His grip was relentless, holding her effortlessly against the wall. Her hands gripped his solid forearm, more for support than survival. One thought ran through her head.

*This man killed your family.*

Dani coughed, clearing her throat. "What's your name?"

"My name is of no importance to you."

"Really? You killed my mother, you slaughtered my father and, worst of all, you blew my little brother's head off. An innocent kid, a kid who never did anyone any harm. I think I earned the fucking right to know your name."

"You father disrespected the code. For that, he had to pay the ultimate price. He knew the consequences."

"What's your fucking *name*?" Dani hissed.

"My name…why? Why is it important? You'll be dead in a minute anyway."

"I want to know who I'm coming for, when I get out of here."

"Really? You'll *come* for me. What makes you think I'll let you live?"

"You would have killed me by now if you were going to. No loose ends means just that. A proper assassin wouldn't stop to converse with a girl just because he gets a fucking boner over the shape of her arse. You're a fucking amateur."

"I'm not an amateur –"

"– you're an amateur. You blew this, pal. You're going down whichever way you look at it. You think with your dick, like most men do, and it's unravelling for you. You don't know it yet...but it is," Dani said, smugly. Her pink, blood-spattered teeth stretched into a smile. Blood glistened on her chin.

Bradley felt sweat tingling his forehead. He knew she couldn't identify him. The hiss in his voice was fake; his clothes covered every inch of his body. He stared at the girl before him. The innocent, yet beautiful, bookworm whose entire body weight rested in just one of his hands, with little to no effort. He had to kill her. Unless...

"A smile, huh? Okay, Danielle. What makes you think you can come and find me?"

"I have my ways."

"Really?"

Dani nodded, licking her lips. Bradley felt the bulge in his trousers once more. He ached to release himself, release inside of her. His eyes, unnoticed behind the shades, eyed her body up and down. She sat on the chest of drawers, her legs spread, enticing him, her chest seemed prominent from this angle. Her arms, bulging with sinew, were clenching his arm, trying to escape. Her slaps only heightened his pleasure. Bradley groaned inwardly, closing his eyes for a split second.

Dani moved, struggling, sensing his weakness.

Bradley realised. *This bitch is smart. Had she spread her legs on purpose?*

Bradley punched Dani in the ribs, winding her. She gasped and went limp beneath his grip.

"I'm intrigued, Danielle. Most women, older, wiser and more experienced, have buckled beneath my demands. Many never lived beyond my visit. You, you *intrigue* me. You want to come and find me, fine. I'm all for sportsmanship. Let's make this interesting."

Dani opened her eyes. The fight ebbed away. "Fuck you," she gasped weakly.

Bradley reached into his pocket and brought out a set of steel kitchen scissors. The gleam of the nightlight caught the wicked, serrated blades. The dark black handles looked sturdy, dangerous.

Dani's eyes widened and she thrashed, once again trying to escape. Bradley smiled beneath his balaclava; he felt the material lift on his sweaty stubble. "I'm all for you coming to find me. Thing is, I have a short term memory for faces," he lied. "So, let me give you something…something that will identify you to me the second you step over my threshold."

Bradley slipped his gloved fingers into the holes on the scissors and worked them open. The blades separated like a pair of steel jaws, the serrated edges glinting in the low light. Dani's eyes widened and she instantly lowered her hands to her stomach and groin, fearing the worst. Bradley chuckled. His hand snapped the blades shut several times, working the mechanism, inciting fear in the young girl. Metallic snaps filled the room.

Dani bucked and thrashed, kicking out at the man who was inches beyond her range. Her legs flailed pointlessly in the air, hitting nothing. Her heels slammed against the chest of drawers, catching the handles, drawing blood beneath her socks. Dani's hands spread over her stomach. She crossed her legs.

Dani gazed at the man, defeated in her struggle, and smiled weakly, no longer scared, wondering if antagonizing this man was sensible. In her eyes, she had lost. Giving up hadn't worked. The next step was death. If she could get him to make a mistake… "Fuck you. Do your worst."

Bradley chuckled again. "I'm so glad you said that. However, my worst is yet to come." The behemoth lifted the scissors, separated the blades, and positioned the crease of Dani's lip between the serrated metal. One, cold blade sat on her tear-stained cheek, the other tickled the inside of the same cheek. Dani tried looking down and found her vision impaired by the darkness and her tears. She could only see the handles of the scissors.

She could feel a lot more though.

Her tongue tasted the cold, metallic intruder in her mouth. Tears welled in her eyes and trickled down her face. Bradley leaned in close. "Are you familiar with a Chelsea grin?"

Dani wanted to shake her head, but fear froze her. Movement could do serious damage. Her eyes spoke volumes and Bradley chuckled again. "You want to come and find me; this will make sure you do. No one forgets a Chelsea grin. It gives you a scar that resembles a permanent smile. Ironic, considering the circumstances. You like smiling at me? After tonight, that's all you'll ever fucking do."

Her eyes glanced down at the weapon, then up again, falling on the intruder once more. He cocked his head. "My name is Bradley. Remember that when you come and find me."

Bradley slowly closed the scissors.

Dani screamed. The serrated blades sliced into her flesh slowly. Every small, serrated tooth pierced soft skin, opening a ragged gash in her cheek, sluicing crimson down her front. Blood exploded in her mouth, trickled down her throat, and Dani began to choke as she felt the crest of her lips split. The tearing of her cheek, the sound of ripping skin and muscle, the vibration of the scissors that reverberated throughout her battered body, made Dani vomit, which exploded from her mouth, down her front and onto the drawers and floor. Her body thrust against the regurgitations, piercing the blades into her cheek even more. White-hot agony crippled her, sending her to the verge of unconsciousness. Her eyes nearly closed.

Bradley withdrew the scissors, the blades gleaming with blood and chunks of flesh and vomit.

He released Dani for a second, realising she could do nothing and go nowhere. Her body was limp, sweating, shaking. Pain had bankrupted her system. He leaned his forearm against her chest just in case. He opened one of the drawers and removed a blue sweater. *Must have belonged to the kid,* he thought. Bradley began wiping the blood from the scissors. He glanced at Dani, impressed. "My, you didn't pass out. Maybe there's hope for you after all."

Dani groaned. Her speech became indecipherable, blood and spit spooling from her mutilated mouth. Bradley noticed her bodily fluids on his forearm and smiled. "Hope, yes. But that was only the first cut."

He readied the scissors again, now clean, and performed the same sequence on Dani's second cheek. Dani didn't put up as much of a fight this time; darkness was on the verge of consuming her. He separated the blades, inserted them into her mouth and began to cut. Dani bucked and thrashed beneath his restraining arm, her body nearly done for. Blood poured from the new hole in her face. A low guttural moan emitted from within the young girl. After a few agonising minutes, he was done. Bradley withdrew the blades and tossed the scissors across the room. They embedded themselves in the wooden doorframe. "There you go. You're now the proud owner of a Chelsea grin."

Dani said nothing, her eyes flickering behind their half-closed lids. Her head wobbled on a weakened neck, her olive skin was a few shades lighter from the blood loss. Bradley held her head up; her slippery chin pinned between two large fingers, and observed his handiwork. She had two slits spreading out from the middle of her mouth, about an inch or so in length. Her chin was a glowing, blood-soaked red. Her clothing, a mass of blood and vomit, would need destroying. Crimson slathered the drawers and floor beneath, as well as the supporting wall behind her. Her kicking and fighting had turned the room into a slaughterhouse.

"Now, for the best bit."

Bradley took a knife from his waistband. Placing it between his teeth, he slapped Dani awake. She murmured, groaning loudly. Her eyes opened slightly, consciousness returning. "Good, you're still with us. When you find me, whenever that might be, I'll be waiting. Next time, I won't be so forgiving." He slid the knife from his mouth, held it before her docile eyes, taunting, and punched it into Dani's waist.

Dani screamed.

Her compromised vermillion crest gave way, the muscles in her mouth stretched and the skin cracked. The flesh split along both cheeks, heading towards the ear. Blood spurted everywhere. Red lines formed and then split – in the shape of a wide, crooked smile – across her face, the skin tearing loudly. Bradley observed his handiwork and laughed. Dani finally passed out from the searing pain.

Bradley dropped her limp, bloody body onto the floor, wiping the blade on the sweater. "You'd better come find me. After this," Bradley gestured to the scene before him, "I'd expect nothing less. You have to survive first though. Good luck."

He took one final look at the carnage, the massacre, and left the room. He walked down the stairs slowly, knocking pictures off the wall as he went and left the house, closing the front door behind him. Within seconds, he was in his vehicle, driving away from the scene.

No one saw him go.

# EIGHT

A sound pierced the air. Faint, at first, but then more striking and obvious.

Dani opened her eyes slowly and winced, her body reacting to the pain. A slow, burning agony spread across her face as exhaustion threatened to engulf her entire body. She gritted her teeth and raised a hand to her lips, stopping an inch from her mutilated visage.

Her tongue licked the inside of her bloody cheek, tasted copper and pulled back. A second time, the probing muscle pushed at the hole in her face. It slid between the slivers of severed flesh, to the outside of her cheek. She licked her clammy skin, tickled by the stifling air in Teddy's bedroom.

It took tremendous willpower not to vomit again.

*What did he do to you?*

The question seemed foolish, the answer obvious, but it gave her clarity, brought her mind back to normality for a second or two. The thought of permanent disfigurement started to enter her mind. She fought it, pushed it down, and scanned the room for a distraction. She saw the door, wide open.

Freedom.

*Get out of here first.*

*You're lucky to be alive. Worry about the damage later.*

She tried to roll over, to no avail. She closed her eyes and focused. Her equilibrium returned and time reset to normal speed. The phantom noise was all too real. The goose bumps on her flesh pricked.

*Was that a siren?*

After a moment, she confirmed it. The sound of a police siren was nearing the house. Its cacophonic sound, one that contained the innate ability to strike fear into the hearts of the criminal, made Dani sit up. The faint blue lights were flickering across the bedroom wall, projected through the window. Teddy's room faced out onto the street, which meant the police were near.

*Is it a trick?*

*Don't be daft.*

Dani heard squeaking hinges. The squeak was high for a second, and then died off. She recognised it instantly. It was her front door. Several footfalls followed.

Coming in, not going out.

Dani took a deep breath, leaned on her right side to avoid crushing her stab wound, and edged towards the open door of the bedroom. Her tongue moved involuntarily to the hole in her face. Dani forced it back to the centre of her mouth and groaned. She felt saliva ooze from the hole and dribble down her ripped cheek. A throbbing pain – dull now, adrenaline was keeping it contained – pulsed through her neck. Her entire head felt like a giant heartbeat.

Dani crawled slowly.

She glanced over at Teddy and felt a sudden loss, a yearning to see her brother one more time, for him to run past her, mocking her. Dani wanted to hear that voice again, just once. All she could see were his legs, his upper body hidden – shrouded in blood-soaked shadows within the wardrobe. Her eyes observed the bloodstains on the carpet, most from her own battered torso. Her arms, legs and front shined dark crimson in the flashing lights. A staggered blood trail smeared the carpet, ending at her waist. She moved her tongue back to the centre of her mouth and composed herself.

This was her fault.

She brought him upstairs.

If they'd headed for the garage – as Dad had suggested – none of this would have happened.

Taking one final look at her dead brother, Dani breathed in, composed herself, and crawled into the hallway. Sweat broke out on her skin, dampening the dried blood there. The severed flesh stung, sending pin pricks of pain into her brain. She stopped and rolled onto her back, exhausted.

"Hello? Anyone here?" A voice in the house beckoned, full of authority.

"Here," her voice came out croaky. She cleared her throat. The newcomer heard it. "We have someone upstairs. Secure the room. Medics!"

Joy washed over Dani, followed by grief and absolute heartbreak. She began crying and sobbing. Seconds later, torchlight illuminated her bloody, broken body. "*Here!*"

One thing was clear.

Bradley was gone.


"Ma'am…I'm Detective Inspector Scott."

Dani looked up at the doorway. She now sat on Teddy's bed. Her shredded face cast pale in the flashlight that scanned the room. After a second, the new arrival turned on the lights, flooding the room with brightness.

Dani flinched, covering her face. Scott took a step forward.

"What's your name, sweetheart?"

"Da…Dani."

"Dani, I'm Mr Scott…you can call me Jack, okay?"

Scott walked into the room, his baton ready, and stopped. His eyes rested on the wardrobe and the massacre within. Teddy's legs were poking out from the doorway - his body face down. Jack glanced from the wardrobe, to Dani and her bloodstained clothing, and breathed out. His eyes settled on her face for the first time.

He saw the wounds, the gashes in her skin, contrasting against her perfect complexion. It looked like she was smiling, a wide smile like a clown, only horribly visceral. Jack narrowed his eyes and realised what he was seeing. His eyes flicked to the bloody scissors embedded in the doorframe, blood dripping from their blades. He lowered his firearm and sighed, then groaned. "Jesus."

Dani didn't look over, didn't respond. She was fighting the pain. Scott flicked his head towards the girl and holstered his weapon. Reaching over, he took the duvet from the bed and wrapped it around Dani, then ushered her to her feet. "I need you to stand up and come with me, can you do that?"

Dani nodded and stood up slowly. She screamed, the stab wound in her waist crippling her, toppling her back to the bed. Scott stepped closer to her, easing her down. "Easy now, easy. Wilson, I need a medic here. *Now!*"

"Did you get the…the guy who did this?"

Scott looked at Dani quizzically.

He observed the blood on her clothes, noticed the gash on her waist. He looked at her bruised face, her battered body, the finger marks on her neck, and wondered what sort of sicko could do this to a teenage girl. He knew then, that he uttered his answer with complete confidence. "Not yet. But we will."

"He was just here though…"

"What?"

"He left…minutes ago. I think."

"You think?"

"I passed out…I could be wrong."

"Main thing is you saw the person who did this." Scott placed a hand on her shoulder. "Wait here." He ran to the landing. "Wilson, put out an APW to the local cars. The guy who did this isn't long gone."

"That's great. Do you have a description?"

Scott averted his gaze to Dani, who coughed and fingered her torn face. "Dressed all in black, armour, balaclava, carrying a shotgun."

Scott nodded. "All black, wearing armour and a balaclava, carrying a shotgun. Worth a shot, put it out. Let's catch the sick fuck who did this. And where's my fucking *medic?*"

Wilson grunted. Muted radio chatter broke the stifled silence.

Scott took Dani by the arm. "You're safe now, Dani. You're safe now."

# NINE

Detective Inspector Scott finished his weak coffee and placed the cup in a bin. Looking at the coffee machine, his hand moved to buy a second cup, remembered the vile taste of the previous one, and stopped.

*You'll be going to the station soon.*

*Maybe hit the coffee shop on the way back.*

He turned around and strode down the hallway, arriving outside the ICU. Several nurses passed with a friendly glance and a curious stare. He paid them no attention and looked through the glass before him. The ward beyond held several ICU patients. His eyes roamed to the far left and settled on Dani. On her arrival, the medical staff had sedated her. Scott had lost track of time, but she now lay silent, covered in bandages and tubes. Several doctors swarmed around her. A couple of nurses stood by, watching, learning.

His heart broke for the young girl.

When he'd found her, she was soaked in blood, most of which was her own. The attacker sliced the young girl's face open with a pair of kitchen scissors and stabbed her, he assumed to initiate the Chelsea grin that now disfigured her. He was familiar with the technique.

Scott remembered a case from last year that showed similar wounds.

The victim, on that occasion, hadn't survived. He was a lot older. Dani had fought valiantly, only passing out in the ambulance on the way here. She'd lost a lot of blood, but she was a fighter. He admired her for that.

Preliminary reports from the crime scene indicated a mass murder. An unknown assailant stormed the household, killed Dani's parents before slaughtering her brother and then torturing her. The torture could have gone on for hours. The kid's bedroom showed signs of struggle and mass bloodletting. Once he figured the brother had died in an enclosed space, he realised just how much blood she'd lost. Scott watched the doctors, their frenzy now controlled, no longer as important or hurried as when they'd arrived.

Dani was safe.

Scott watched TV shows. In emergencies, people shouted words like *'stat'* and *'clear'* and a variety of medical jargon, usually accompanied by paddles or fancy gadgets if something serious was going on. That wasn't happening here. Everything was calm. Scott didn't expect the TV shows to be accurate at all, but he took it as a good sign that everything was running quietly. People weren't panicking; they were in control.

He placed his thumbs in his pockets and flattened his palms on his thighs. After a second, he started drumming with them, calming himself.

*You may have saved the girls life tonight, but at what cost?*

He'd seen the scars, the damage, and the tragic loss that followed her to that hospital bed. When she walks out of here, she'll have nothing.

Her family is gone. Next of kin was yet to be determined, but he held out little hope of that being a structured future for the girl. He wasn't an expert, but he remembered his sister as a teenager growing up. For a teenage girl, image was everything if the hour-long showers, his father's credit card bills and the expensive make-up habit was to go by.

He remembered arguing with his sister, on countless occasions, because she'd used all the hot water or taken all of the dry towels. His sister didn't have two holes in her face either, or a trail of corpses in her past. Scott scratched his forehead, feeling the frown lines.

On top of that, her attackers might come back.

He'd have to make sure that didn't happen.

How?

He wasn't sure yet.

Only she would ever know what happened to her that night. He wouldn't question her about it unless absolutely necessary. Right now, he knew Dani's future relied on one person.

Him.

Scott rubbed his face with both palms. When he lowered them, a nurse exited the room, looked around, and walked towards him. He feigned a smile.

"Detective Inspector?"

"Yes, please, call me Jack."

The nurse said nothing and looked down at her notes, confirming her information. Without looking up, she spoke. "Detective Inspector, you brought the girl in, is that right?"

"That's right," Scott said, perplexed. *Didn't she know this?*

"Did you come straight from her home?"

"I did, she was found at her home, a crime scene. She's the only survivor."

The nurse frowned. "Only survivor?"

"Yes, the investigation is ongoing."

"The girl is in a terrible state. You probably noticed, she has three, very dangerous lacerations. Infection is a high probability due to the proximity of the wounds to her mouth, but we've run a course of antibiotics to be safe. We'll have to monitor her in the meantime. We've treated the bruises and the minor injuries, but she's in bad shape."

Scott nodded.

"The wounds on her face were made with a pair of kitchen scissors. They're in a plastic bag for evidence. The third wound, the one on her waist, was done by a knife." Scott smiled, trying to help. "Well, that's what we assume. We haven't found the weapon yet."

"Assume?"

"By the width of the puncture wound and the angle at which the weapon was thrust, one I've seen a hundred times before, indication points to a small knife."

"You examined her?" The nurse queried.

"No, her top was shredded…the wound was visible on the way here. I rode in the ambulance with her as the medics tried to stabilise her."

"Seems like you should come and work for us," the nurse smiled. "You're familiar with the term Chelsea smile? Or Glasgow grin? Or a variation of either?"

"I am indeed."

"Do you have any reason to suspect this is a gang related incident?"

"I can't say."

"Mob related?"

"Again, I can't say. We haven't processed the information yet."

The nurse made some notes on her clipboard.

"When can I speak to her?" Scott said calmly, knowing the answer before it escaped the nurse's lips.

"That won't be possible yet. We just sedated her; she's in a very bad way. She'll require surgery, a consultation with the max fac doctor –"

"– I'm sorry, what?"

"Max fac…I'm sorry, the maxillofacial doctors. This girl, Danielle is it? She'll need surgery to ensure the nerve endings in her cheeks are corrected properly. The lacerations compromised the vermillion crest – that's the red part of your lips – and the nasolabial fold, so the doctor needs to line that up perfectly. The procedure is very delicate, but essential.

This girl has been through enough without having lopsided lips, and permanent disfiguration, for the rest of her life. As it stands, you could fit your entire fist in her mouth right now. The severity of the injuries is immense. She survived this; let's make it as painless as possible."

Scott gulped.

The thought of it terrified him. *Poor kid.*

The nurse continued writing. Scott drummed his thighs again. "When do you think she'll be able to talk?"

The nurse thrust her clipboard down with such vehemence; it made Scott flinch. Her eyes glared at him. "Detective Inspector, pardon my manners, but this girl has been through a horrific ordeal. You noticed the wounds on her face? It'll be some time before she can talk. She needs surgery, stitches and probably speech therapy before talking is even commonplace for her. On top of that, she'll need to learn how to chew and eat, swallow. She'll need rehabilitation on her face muscles. This girl has a massive undertaking ahead of her. I couldn't give you a timeline on that, but please respect the fact that your investigation will have to *wait*. Excuse me."

The nurse walked away. Scott rubbed his face again. He slipped his mobile phone from his pocket and dialled. After a moment, the call clicked on.

"Wright."

"It's Scott. Listen, the girl is in bad shape, but she won't be speaking for a while. Any updates on the crime scene?"

"We're still processing the evidence. This place is a slaughterhouse. Initial conclusion is that one person did it. We should have something concrete in a few hours."

"No worries."

"Scott, if you want to catch this guy, we really need her testimony to get a clearer picture. Our dicks are swinging in the wind here."

"Guess I'll hang around then. Keep at it and call me if anything changes. Laters."

Scott hung up and slid the phone back into his pocket. He walked down the hallway and fed some coins into the coffee machine. He sighed, observing the empty seats in the waiting room. He wondered how comfortable they'd be.

It could be a long night.

# TEN

Dani drummed her fingers on the metal table before her. The torturous images of her once safe and comfortable home were dancing erratically behind her eyes, slowly scarring her brain and innocence forever.

She thought back to that night, two months ago.

The images were still crystal clear in her mind's eye. It's why Jack Scott had instructed her to close her eyes on their exit from the crime scene.

She hadn't.

After her own personal hell, and having her brother's brain splattered all over her, she wanted to see everything else.

Whether it was a wise decision or not, only time would tell.

Moments later, they closed on their own as she passed out in the ambulance. The next two months were mostly a drug-riddled blur as various doctors and nurses healed her and saved her life. Dani would be forever grateful.

The memories stayed put though.

The sight of her mother, her chest tattered and torn by buckshot from a shotgun shell, was horrific. There was crimson everywhere; on the floors, the walls, the furniture and the ceiling.

However, the blood spots that decorated her mother's face pushed her over the edge. For some reason, seeing her mother's innocent, beautiful visage slathered in blood and terror was one of the worst sight of her years so far.

A sheet obscured her father's corpse. Only his left hand, poking out from the sheet at an obscure angle, was visible. His injuries were a mystery, unknown. She aimed to find out what happened though. In due course.

The holding cell she sat in was minimal, chilly. A huge, fluffy fleece covered her shoulders. Dani tugged at her ponytail, which sat low on her head. She normally wore it a lot higher, but it was useful for the rehabilitation, so she'd become accustomed. Hair no longer hung in her face, it only caused the doctor and nurses hassle on her multiple appointments and cleansings. Plus, Dani didn't like when the hair caught the scar tissue on her cheeks. It was irritable. The ponytail made life much simpler.

Her tongue gently probed the inside of her mouth. She felt the dissolvable sutures there, newly applied. The bandages on her face covered the worst, but she knew the wounds existed. She pushed it from her mind.

After a minute, Jack Scott walked into the room, smiled, and closed the door behind him. He placed a manila file, topped with a box of cigarettes and a Zippo, before her on the table. Dani didn't know how the police worked, but she knew she wasn't under arrest. She hadn't done anything wrong. They just had some questions.

Jack leaned forward. "I'm sorry about your loss. I can't imagine what you're going through." Dani just stared at him, her gaze lost and wandering, focusing on nothing. He sighed, and slipped a cigarette from the pack before him. He held them out to Dani, saw the damage to her face, realised his error, and withdrew sheepishly.

Dani said nothing.

Scott remembered how frail Dani had been after that night. He looked her up and down, placed his cigarette back into the pack and placed it on the desk. He topped it with the Zippo lighter, confirming his will to wait.

He had no idea what rehabilitation had happened, but he wasn't about to jeopardise it by smoking.

Dani stared ahead, past Jack's left shoulder.

"There's no real way to say this without sounding inappropriate…How are you, Dani? You doing okay?"

Dani diverted her withered gaze to Scott and nodded.

"Off the record, you're not in any trouble. We just want to generate an idea of what happened at your home and to…your family." Jack coughed. "You ready?"

Dani nodded, silent.

"Are you able to speak?"

Dani nodded.

"Does it hurt to talk? I have a pad here if it's easier."

Dani paused for a second and held out a hand, refusing the pad.

"Okay, whenever you're ready. Short answers are fine. No rush, take your time."

"Shall I starts at the beginninush?" Dani's words were slurred slightly, normal according to the speech therapist. She hadn't spoken much in the past few months and realised the words would correct themselves in time. If her cheeks tugged when she spoke, they'd advised to stop. She eyed the pad, thinking it might have been a better idea after all.

"The beginning is good. Gives us a clearer picture," Scott smiled.

Dani told him everything she knew.

How their evening was plodding along. Dinner, family banter, doing her homework, Teddy's irritating mannerisms. At the last one, Dani choked and began to cry. Instant guilt swarmed through her chest, making her cough. She kept her mouth shut, protecting the stitches as the coughs jostled her body.

Jack handed her a pack of tissues. Dani took two and wiped her mouth. She sat back, pulling the fleece closer.

Jack watched the young girl, his eyes observing her body language.

He opened the file on the metal table, unsure of how to proceed. Dani paid him no attention and closed her eyes. He swallowed, breathed in and went for it.

"We couldn't find the people...person who did this."

Dani remained silent, did nothing.

"I apologise. We will catch them."

Again, no reaction.

"The investigation is at a standstill. We thought your testimony would shed light on something we haven't found, but we did a thorough job. If we could find the attacker, if we knew who he was or what he did –"

"You won't catch him," Dani uttered, not moving.

Jack stopped, frowning slightly. "Excuse me?"

Dani opened her eyes, the pupils raging behind the tears and blood-shot whites. They penetrated Jack's soul, made him flinch a little. "You won't catch him."

Jack shuffled forward. "How do you know?"

Dani felt a smirk tugging at her sutures, surprising herself with the response. She cleared her throat. "He was wearing all black. I mean all; every inch of his body was covered. DNA, fingerprints, sweat, saliva, you wouldn't have got any. The guy was *smart*. He walked in, not a care in the world and slaughtered my family. He would have killed me if..." Dani didn't finish the sentence. A thought popped into her mind.

"We were alerted by the sound of gunshots. Your neighbors called it in."

Dani looked down. *Thank you, Mrs Jones*. She instantly regretted it. The thought of losing Teddy made her wish she'd gone with him. *If I'd stepped out of that wardrobe first, everything might have been different.* Or she could have gone straight after him, let the guy take both of them out. She could protect him in the afterlife. She'd take his pestering all day long if she could just see him one more time. Fresh tears rolled down her cheek, blotting her bandages. She hugged the fleece closer.

Seeing her response, Jack sat back again. "I'm sorry," he uttered across the table.

Dani closed her eyes and nodded once. She knew what was coming next.

"Have you got someone you can stay with?"

"Yeah, I have an aunt I can go to," Dani lied.

"I bet you'll be glad to get out of that hospital?"

Dani nodded. In honesty, the thought of leaving the safe sanctuary terrified her.

"I'll make some calls."

Dani stood up. "Don't call my aunt, she doesn't have...well, she lives in the Stone Age. The telephone terrifies her. I'll go over there now."

"Need a lift?"

"No...I think I want to walk for a bit. Being cooped up in a hospital really inspires you to get some fresh air. I've missed the outdoors."

"So be it," Scott said. He looked up at the girl, a girl who'd lost everything in a few short hours, some months ago. He wanted to provide her some hope. "We'll catch this fucker, Dani, I promise."

Jack stood up, taking the folder with him. Dani watched him go.

She wasn't the only liar in the room. Jack exited, closing the door silently.

Dani snuggled into the fleece.

She had work to do.


Dani sniffled as she watched the jaundiced CRIME SCENE tape flutter in the wind. The faded plastic spooled across her front garden, wrapped around three spaced out railings along the street. A staggered rectangle, cordoning off the house to any nosy reporters or prying eyes.

*Yeah, like it could stop anyone from ducking underneath.*

A separate, shorter stretch – snapped in the middle – clung to the red front door. Someone had passed through, probably Jack or another officer doing his duty.

A pit of sadness and isolation opened up in her stomach as she turned from the house, realising she would never step foot within again. Her entire life, every memory in her home, was dropping through a blood-soaked void.

Dani pulled the fleece around her shoulders and limped towards the garage. She lifted the metal shutter slowly, wincing as the stab wound scorched her entire body with sudden pain, and fished the BMW key from her pocket. Her finger squeezed the little padlock icon on it and an electronic thump emitted from the car.

She walked around to the boot.

With one hand, she lifted the lid slowly. The fresh smell of carpet rose from within. Dani remembered her father buying the car weeks before the incident, remembered how excited he'd been. If Dani were capable, she would have smiled at the happy memory. Instead, she rubbed her face cautiously, feeling the scars beneath the protective bandages.

*Will I ever be able to smile properly again?*

Dani looked into the boot and saw nothing of importance. Grey carpet, a bottle of antifreeze and a wheel jack. She frowned as the memory resurfaced slowly.

She smacked her left hand against the side of the boot, whapping against a padded panel. The carpet in the middle of the boot lifted slightly, exposing a hidden, rectangular crevice.

Two months ago, maybe more, her father had done the same thing. He hadn't been aware of her presence and she'd kept it to herself.

After all, boys and their toys.

She knew men spent a lot of time on their cars, adding modifications, installing sound systems and all sorts of fancy gadgets.

A hidden panel was unusual.

Whilst in the police station, everything fell into place. Dani felt relief that she hadn't revealed this to DI Scott. After obtaining the key from her father, who insisted it was for her to drive, she'd become suspicious.

Driving lessons weren't in her immediate plans; she didn't have time or need for them, which struck her as odd. Walking was good for her, it enabled her to think, alone and undisturbed, and to seek solace in her headphones. Why drive when you can walk and not only save money, but also be productive in the meantime? Sure, she'd been ecstatic, who doesn't like receiving a car, but something was off about the gift.

That's when Dani realised something else was afoot.

Due to the rehabilitation, antibiotics, and surgery, none of this occurred to Dani until a few days ago. Her foggy mind kept the revelation from her until, at the right time; the fog vanished and left her with the answer. Her tongue probed the scars again, out of habit.

Dani sat on the workbench behind her, realisation dawning. Her father *knew* they were coming for him. He hadn't warned them, or done anything to protect his family. Dani choked back tears, thinking of Teddy and her mother, innocent lambs to the slaughter. A simple drive and they could've stayed in a cabin or hotel somewhere, safe and sound.

A simple drive and none of this would have happened.

*Damn you, Dad, damn you.*

Dani stood up, gently wiping the tears from her face. After a second, she lifted the panel and exposed a hollow. Inside sat a dark brown, wooden box, about the size of a small DVD player. Lifting her head to check if the coast was clear – which it was – Dani collected the box and slid it into her bag. She checked the hidden compartment once more and shut it.

She closed the boot and took her mobile phone from her pocket. She had no messages and no missed calls.

That was about to change. She expected relatives to emerge from the woodwork, pound signs flashing in their deceitful and gluttonous eyes.

She hadn't heard from any of her aunts or uncles in nearly a decade. With her father being wealthy, she expected this to change.

She was the only point of contact.

"Dani?"

Narrowing her eyes, Dani stepped around the car, pushing the boot closed as she did. When she reached the driver's side, she saw a familiar face standing at the opening to the garage. Two months ago, her heart would have sunk. Now, she didn't give a shit. A lot had happened since that horrible afternoon. Nothing he could do or say would ever ruin her life, not anymore. Not now it was practically taken from her.

"Hello, Ben."

Her former boyfriend stood awkwardly, tense, backlit by the murky sky. His left hand wavered in the air, as if wanting to shake hands with her, as if some inner turmoil prevented him from stretching the limb. As Dani neared him, his face came into focus. A sheepish grin adorned it, spread below twinkling eyes. Dani felt nothing, didn't respond. Aware that the dark shadows from the garage shrouded her, masked her injuries; she stopped moving, concealing herself. Dani remained silent, awaiting a response.

"How are you?"

Dani said nothing.

"It's been a while. I called and texted, you didn't reply."

A rage boiled within Dani. Her fingers tightened around her phone, the inactive phone that revealed Ben as an outright liar. The phone squeaked as her fingers threatened to crack the device. "Why are you here?"

"I came to say –"

"–what, you're sorry? Pardon me if I find that hard to believe."

"I am, though. I heard about what happened…" Ben looked at the house, the dull structure that once bustled with life and light. Now, it stood like a forgotten abode, soaked in despair and misery.

Ben's eyes scrolled to the front door and he remembered kissing Dani goodnight on the doorstep on numerous occasions. He smiled.

Dani noticed the smile and immediately knew what he was thinking. Despite their disagreements – *his disagreement, after all, he's the cheating fucker* – she remembered the memory fondly.

Forbidden teenage love. Exciting, passionate, monitored closely by caring, nosy parents. Ben never stepped foot in her house at her father's insistence.

*Weird,* she thought.

None of that mattered now.

Dani took a step forward, emerging from the protective shadow of the garage. "You didn't come here to say sorry."

Ben turned to her, his eyes taking in the damage on Dani's face and he gasped, backing away. Dani's eyes narrowed, her lips pursed in a tight line. "You came here to have a nosy, didn't you? You wanted to be the first to see the freak. I'll bet that Chantelle put you up to this?"

"I had to see it for myself. I didn't believe the story. One day, you were here and the next, your whole family is gone. I thought you might have moved."

Dani stepped towards Ben, peeling away her bandages slowly. "My family were murdered. *Murdered!* It featured in every newspaper from here to outer fucking Mongolia, so don't tell me you didn't believe it. You saw it for yourself. I know you can read. It was one of the few things I admired about you."

Ben, a slight smile on his face, came towards Dani. His eyes roamed her face, the puffy, pale skin, the scars that angled towards both ears, contrasting against her natural olive shade. The sides of her lips angled outwards, the swelling still present. Black, sleep deprived rings circled Dani's eyes. Her complexion, where normally perfect, was blemished and gaunt. Her hair still sat in an unkempt ponytail.

Ben stopped. "Chantelle didn't send me."

"Bullshit," Dani spat.

"She didn't."

"Morbid curiosity was never your strong point. You hate getting involved in things like this. She put you up to coming here.

Probably wants an update for her blog or something."

"I came to see if you were okay."

Dani paused. A sense of sincerity tinged his voice. She almost fell for it. His betrayal tinted every word. "I want you to leave."

"I came for you."

"Yeah, well, if you weren't such a cheating bastard, you might have the fucking right to do so. You have no idea what you did to me that day. I had to walk home and find my boyfriend, the guy who told me to ignore my parents warnings, the boy who confessed his love to me, playing tonsil tennis with another girl. A slag, nonetheless. Kissing isn't cheating? Isn't that what a whore would say to a client? What sort of deluded world does she live in?"

"Dani —"

"— I don't want to hear it, Ben. I learned one thing from you and that is to trust no one. We're done. After today, you won't be seeing me again."

She turned and walked back into the garage.

"Dani?"

"Fuck off."

Dani dropped her phone on the floor and kicked it behind the dusty workbench in the corner. She watched Ben struggle with his emotions, his lack of chance to get a photograph — she'd seen him slide the phone from his pocket, hesitant to snap her hideous visage — and eventually, he walked off the driveway and home, vanishing from sight. He'd bottled it, as always. She wondered how Chantelle would react to his failure.

*Good riddance*, she thought.

Dani opened the driver door and climbed in. The leather squeaked beneath her rump. She slipped the key into the ignition and turned the car on, thumbing the radio off.

Slowly, she pulled out of the garage and turned into the road, snapping the CRIME SCENE tape.

Dani didn't look at the house as she drove the car away from her entire past.

Leaving her home and the horrific memories behind.

A moment later, her mobile phone vibrated on the concrete floor.

It remained unanswered.

# PART TWO

## Best Laid Plans

# ELEVEN

## ONE YEAR LATER

Bradley blew out a stream of acrid cigarette smoke and casually observed.

He liked to observe, it relaxed him.

Observing was a preferred pastime of his, something he thoroughly enjoyed. Bradley had never been one for video games, TV, poker, or anything that helped pass a person's mundane existence. He felt it spoiled the cognitive function, caused distractions. Bradley didn't like to be distracted; in his line of work, it could be fatal.

He liked music, but that was something else entirely.

Distractions denied focus, they stunted organisation. He couldn't have that.

No, Bradley preferred to be organised. For forty long years, he had been prepared; ready for anything and poised for nothing to go wrong. It made him a valuable asset to anyone who knew him. As a result, he was also extremely dangerous.

A prepared man is essentially a deadly one.

He finished his cigarette, tossed the butt in the fireproof bin to his left, and pulled the heavy iron door open. A wave of heat gushed out, warming his wind-bitten face. Bradley stepped through the door and let it shut behind him.

He closed his eyes and took in the smells, breathed in deeply. The perfumes, the sweat, the food, and odors of normal everyday activity. Bradley opened his eyes. He stepped forward and walked through a wooden archway.

Once through, he paused.

He liked to observe, it relaxed him.

The concourse before him bore little resemblance to its former life as a basketball court. The concrete floor still stood proud, yes, and the worn red and blue markings of the various zones relevant to the sport still divided the concrete into useless sections. The hoops were still secured high up in the air, suspended on rusted metal arms. They retracted far into the ceiling; there was no use for them now. The nets hung awkwardly, leaning against the dusty metal rims. Bradley smiled, remembering his youth. He played basketball once or twice. He recalled being quite good at it, but boxing was more his sport. He almost went pro.

The court divided into areas, with each area providing a home to two mobile cabins. Bradley didn't count, but he knew there were sixteen units, eight areas in total. The units were green and basic and the windows wired up, the type of units you see on building sites, to occupy the staff on lunch breaks. He'd been on a few sites in his time so he knew the feeling. Cold, stinking of coffee or tea, and being crammed into them like sardines with all of your workmates. Trading soggy sandwiches and anecdotes, slandering the wives and cheating girlfriends behind their backs.

It wasn't a feeling he wished to relive.

These modified units were home to a number of women. Bradley knew they currently had twenty working girls on their books. They had a rotation system, which meant each woman occupied one cabin at a time. The four remaining women were working, bringing in the money. Bradley knew the money was a reasonable amount. It kept him in work and very comfortably at that. He owned an Audi, rented a plush, minimal apartment, and wore a Rolex.

Times were good.

Bradley walked across the court and idled between two units. Closed doors meant the women were sleeping, resting after their multiple performances of the day. Strict rotation meant that Thursday was a quiet day. Two or three performances meant that the women rested for a few hours in between each. They would probably have the whole night to themselves, locked away in their units, counting their takings or patching themselves up. They could do whatever kept them happy.

Bradley knew that each woman had access to a bed, a bookshelf, a TV fed from a main switcher box upstairs, and toilet and medical facilities. They had comforts, but they had to realise they were there to work. In addition, they had to take the chance to rest; the weekends were usually hectic. Married customers could feign business trips during the week, but many wouldn't risk it until the weekend. It meant they were less restricted, freer with their earnings. Bradley smiled at the idea of marriage. Nowadays, it seemed more like a hindrance than an actual tradition.

He had heard that fifty percent of marriages ended in divorce, many in their early years.

*Why bother?* Bradley found himself shaking his head.

He moved on. As he strolled, he brushed his fingertips along the coarse cabin walls. Possibly feeling for movement inside, mostly out of routine. The cold, anti-corrosive paint felt fresh and smooth beneath his fingertips. He closed his eyes, savouring the touch, the cool feeling.

*The simple things are best, so many take them for granted*, he thought.

After a moment, he reached the double doors that occupied the right side of the court.

Beyond the doors lay the business centre of Rhodes' little empire. He took one final glance at the cabins, studied each for two seconds, smiled when content, and turned around. Bradley stepped through the double doors and waited. He could hear faint music on the air. A recent song, familiar, one he'd heard numerous times, but couldn't recall the name or artist.

Not one of the greats, not one he would find in his music collection. Nothing as classic as Holly or Springsteen or Clapton.

Bradley was in an aqua blue hallway, which was home to a number of marked doorways. Between each doorway, hanging on the wall, was a painting. Bradley was not a fan of art and didn't know the paintings by name or painter. There was one with a tree. Another with a screaming man. A third with a man standing on a dock, staring out to sea. All very elegant. They seemed like pieces picked out of a catalogue for their convenience or popularity rather than for their tradition. It gave the hallway a welcoming, but tidy appeal. Bradley knew people didn't come here for the scenery outside of the rooms anyway. He smiled and strode down the corridor.

A door burst open behind him. Bradley spun casually and saw a woman collapse to the carpet. She was naked bar a small black thong, one mostly hidden in the cleft of her shapely behind. Her legs had folded up beneath her. Her mane of dark hair covered her face and shoulders, and her arms crossed defensively, covering small breasts with dark nipples. She spun to face the door and threw her arms out, hands spread, in an attempt to shield her from whatever was coming after her.

The girl was sobbing.

A man emerged behind her. He wore a dark red robe that hung open in the middle, his pale, hairy gut protruding from between the material. His expensive white boxers did nothing to hide his throbbing erection. In one hand, he held a tumbler of amber liquid.

Whiskey or bourbon? Bradley couldn't tell. The other hand was trying to grab the woman by the hair. She was cowering away, yelping.

Bradley recognised the girl as Britney.

It was her nineteenth birthday today, which meant this was her solitary shift for the day, a gift from Rhodes himself, one bestowed on all the girls. She was Brazilian-American, which gave her a special foreign appeal. International flavour, high in demand, and very expensive.

In his eyes, Britney was the most beautiful woman they had on the payroll. Unfortunately, because of her age she was also quite naïve. It was obvious the customer was trying it on, taking advantage, and Britney was having none of it.

Bradley stepped forward and made a mental note of the room number. After a second, he approached the man. He said nothing, simply lingering in the man's peripheral view. The man became aware of his presence and looked at him. Only then did Bradley smile. "Problem, sir?" He had his arms folded behind his back. He resembled a bouncer outside a nightclub.

"Yeah, this whore won't let me fuck her in the arse." The man jabbed at the air violently, gesturing towards the sky, the drink sloshing in his other hand. Britney was receding into the wall. Any further and she would probably vanish into it.

Bradley continued smiling.

"I apologise sir, but as you can see you are in B-Wing. Room fourteen is for our basic customers, sir. You haven't paid for anything other than basic sex, normal sexual positions and a bit of cheeky fellatio. I call it our amateur package, for beginners if you will. Britney is simply abiding by our strict rules and doing her job. Please don't put me in a position to use force here, okay?"

"But I want to fuck her in the arse, it shouldn't cost extra. What sort of fucking Mickey Mouse operation do you run here?"

The man looked appalled.

"Do you have your membership card, sir?"

The man glared at Bradley. After a long second, he stepped back into the room with a huff. He returned with his wallet and handed it to Bradley. It was fat and full of cash, the strained leather bulging with paper and credit cards. More credit than a man could need, or want, the sign of a man consumed by greed and power.

A man who felt entitled to anything he wanted.

Bradley shook his head. It wasn't how this operation did business. He flipped open the wallet and slipped out a silver membership card, recognising the familiar insignia in the left corner.

*RR.* He tossed the wallet back to the man, who grunted as it slapped him in on his bulging cheek. Bradley inspected the membership card. Embossed letters spelt the man's name. It shone in the light.

"Bernard, may I call you Bernard?"

"No you may not; my name is Dr. Bernard Buck. Dr. Buck to you, okay? May I have my card back?"

"Bernard. For that little spat, I will now refer to you as arsehole. Dr. Arsehole, just so we are on the same fucking level here. You, *Dr. Arsehole*, have a silver membership card. That entitles you to – I hope you're listening – basic amenities. Rooms ten to fourteen only, which means basic sex as I mentioned. You can fuck, you can get your dick sucked and you can fulfill any boring, sexual position that your wife won't allow. Allow or finds repulsive, after all, look at the state of you, you fat cunt."

Bernard's eyes bulged and widened, his mouth hung agape.

Bradley continued.

"However, you will *not* be fucking Britney in the arse; you will not be grabbing her by the hair because that constitutes BDSM and rough sex, which is way beyond your membership quota and, finally, you certainly will not be arguing with me on this. We don't run a Mickey Mouse show here, if you want that, you can fuck off to Disneyland like a proper little nonce.

We have a professional business here, and if you cannot abide by the rules, then your membership will be terminated, are we clear?"

Bernard was silent. His erection had subsided, probably because the blood has rushed to his face. His mottled cheeks were bright crimson. Clearly, no one had spoken to him like that in years, possibly ever. He seemed like a man who did what he wanted when he wanted. He finished his amber liquid, the glass trembling between his chubby fingers, clinking on his wedding band, and went back into his room. Moments later, he returned with his suitcase and hat. He looked absurd.

He still wore the red gown, in addition to leather loafers and his boxers. A sheen of sweat illuminated his large forehead below the lights. He stomped off down the hallway.

He stopped and looked back at Bradley.

Bradley was still smiling.

"Off you fuck, go on!"

Bernard turned and walked away, slamming the door behind him.

After a moment, Bradley bent down to Britney. She was still cowering away. He swept her hair back to make sure she was okay. Britney stared up at him in terror, eyes wide. Bradley lingered on her eyes for a second before helping her up. She truly was beautiful, despite the black eye she had recently acquired.

*Beautiful.*

*Just like her.*

*Just like Danielle.*

Bradley flinched, backing away.

*I haven't thought about her in months,* he thought.

When she was on her feet, Britney nodded sheepishly, stared at the floor and walked into the room, closing the door behind her.

Bradley stared at the door, placing his palm flat against it, and then pulled his mobile phone from his pocket. Cursing, he dialed a number and waited. After a muted second, there was a click on the phone.

"We have a problem. We have a customer who overstepped his boundary. What shall I do?"

The voice on the other end said, "Whatever is necessary".

Bradley snapped his phone shut.

He closed his eyes and smiled. This was the favorite part of his job. He removed his hand from the door. Thirty seconds later, he was walking down the hall.

*Dr. Bernard Buck, forty-four and overweight, married with no children. Found dead in a ditch the next morning.*

*They found his severed tongue deep in his anus.*

*The fingers and toes were missing. They found his wallet, his credit cards and his hat in his engorged belly. A terrible mess. They found his wife at home, a gouge where her throat had once been. The missing fingers and toes were scattered around her corpse. The neighbors said they had been a normal couple; the husband was always away on business. Mrs. Buck has been an exemplary social figure. The events were a mystery.*

Bradley blew out a stream of cigarette smoke, pocketed his pen and closed his notebook. He wondered how long it would be before the press printed that article, with little or no detail.

*The sack of shit had it coming. He made me think of her...of Danielle.*

Bradley closed his eyes, cleared his thoughts.

*No distractions, you know the rules.*

*Observe – that'll calm you down.*

He liked to observe, it relaxed him.

He liked to problem solve even more so.

He closed his eyes, pushing the memory of the lovely Danielle from his brain – *after all, she was dead, no one could survive that attack, especially a teenager* – and smiled.

*She's dead. It's been over a year. Forget her.*

# TWELVE

Corey Cross, Alan Cahill, Jorge Sanchez, and Philip Andrews, the lackeys.

Bradley Innis; the right hand man. The man who killed her family and mutilated her.

Their boss, Ross Rhodes.

Dani scanned her weary eyes down the piece of paper in her hand, the off-white sheet crinkled from multiple handlings over the past year.

It held six names, the six responsible for her family's demise. Her father had scrawled them in red ink, neatly and tightly. It detailed their activity and their respective role in their organisation, the organisation her father had worked for until his brutal murder.

His name was next to Corey and Alan, a solid black line through it.

Her handiwork.

After all, he was dead now.

Face facts.

He wasn't coming back to help her.

Dani grunted and sat up. The mattress beneath her creaked as she adjusted her lithe frame. She placed the list on her bedside cabinet next to her parent's platinum wedding rings, linked together via a small silver chain.

Her smooth, tanned legs rolled over and her sock covered feet plodded onto the laminate floor. She crossed her apartment, wearing only a pair of blue panties and a sports bra – and the socks – and entered her walk-in shower, a concrete rectangle with a wet floor and wall. She slipped her garments off and tossed them into the hamper, walked behind the partition and started to shower.

Every morning the same.

Washing the tragedy off her skin.

She ran the water to near boiling, until she felt her skin object to the level of heat and stayed there for eleven minutes, as she did every morning. The tingle of searing pain crawled beneath her skin. Her scars itched beneath the heat. Two seconds had extended to thirty seconds and that had extended to one minute, then two, then three. Gradually, over the next year, she'd extended her mini ordeal to eleven full minutes. This time, she didn't flinch. A murky mist rose around her. Dani inhaled, clearing her sinuses with a deep lungful of steam. Her back became numb under the scorching water. Still, she didn't flinch.

Not once.

A year ago, she'd have cried tears and probably ran cold water over the burned area immediately.

Now, no such action was necessary.

Progress.

After all, routine was important.

As was discipline.

Emerging from the shower with hot, pink skin, she wrapped a towel around her, tucked it at the side of her breasts, and walked to her desk. She booted up her laptop and sat down. Her eyes flicked to the brown box on the desk beside her and her mind wandered.

She had time.

A year ago, her BMW ride had taken her away from Nowheresville to a small town in Kent called Royal Tunbridge Wells. It was the first destination on her father's GPS and a stone's throw from London. Her father worked exclusively in the capital, but not for a software firm as his ruse had confirmed.

It was a little more sinister than that.

She'd since learned he was working for the mob.

It had gotten her family killed. Over the past year, she'd come to forgive her father, despite his actions in getting those she loved slaughtered.

After all, he'd just wanted to give them a good life. College, education, loving parents.

Dani dropped out of college immediately following the massacre. The physical scars were too much, her mind too fragile and broken to concentrate on education. Her mutilated face was all over the news for four months following the attack. Going to college was not an option; her meeting with Ben all but confirmed that. A day later, she cut her hair, dyed it, and purchased a baseball cap. A suitable disguise. She'd also invested in some snoods, which made covering her face much easier. People didn't seem to notice her so much after that.

Dani gazed at the box on the sofa, the one she'd retrieved from her father's vehicle.

The first items in the box had been a credit card and a debit card. The credit card was set up in a fake name. She cut it up and tossed it immediately. The debit card was in Dani's name, the balance just over a million pounds. The money was dirty; there was no doubt about it. She didn't care. Money wouldn't bring her family back, but it would help her find those responsible for their deaths.

The box also contained the list she'd read every morning for the past three hundred and sixty five days. It contained her parent's wedding rings – surprisingly, she'd not noticed they weren't wearing them – and a heap of documents and diaries detailing her father's illegal activities. It had been difficult reading. Her father has been a murderer, a gun for hire.

Which explained the final two items.

Two Beretta handguns – complete with clips, a box of bullets and suppressors. Dani wasn't familiar with firearms, but she knew, by UK law, that they were illegal.

After doing some research, she discovered Berettas were standard police issue in other European countries, which made access to them simple – for criminals anyway.

After a lengthy training course, reading up on the ammunition types, suppressor functions, and maintenance procedures, she'd adopted them as her own. She relished the day she could use them. Her eyes flicked to the list on the bedside.

She ran the mantra through her head. *Her father had been a murderer, a gun for hire.*

*A murderer.*

*A gun for hire.*

Apparently, he wasn't very good at it.

Teddy and her mother were testament to that.

Dani uncurled the damp towel from her hair and ran it through her damp locks. She flicked her head back and heard her soggy hair slap her bare shoulders. For a moment, she ran her fingertips through the locks, remembering when she'd cut them a year ago, remembering with no fondness the dry, rough strands that made her scalp itch. She pushed them against her face, savouring their damp feel, smelling her candy shampoo.

She shook her head.

*No, not now. You've spent a year getting away from your past.*

Dani ran her hands through her hair, tucking it behind her ears, and sighed. She then removed the towel and dried her slick body.

She dropped and did fifty press-ups. Then, she rolled over, onto her back, and did fifty sit-ups. Finally, she stood up and did fifty pull-ups in the doorframe, using its rim for support. Her muscles ached and burned, her fingers tingled. Dani looked down at her naked, sweat-covered body and smiled gently, her fingertips caressing the mounds of scar tissue on both sides of her mouth.

A year had gone into her preparation.

At first, Dani didn't know the goal, the objective. As she'd built herself up through exercise, discipline, and research, the goal slowly became clear to her. Tears no longer spilled.

She'd kept Teddy's duvet to this day, but it no longer emoted the feelings it had in the aftermath of the massacre. Even looking in the mirror didn't have the same effect anymore. Initially, she couldn't look at her reflection; tears were automatic on seeing her visage. Now, she didn't give it a second thought, merely turning the emotion into rage, a rage she buried deep. When the time came, it would emerge. Every time she stroked the scar lines in her face, it fuelled her, added to the vengeance building within.

She'd evolved. She no longer saw Danielle.

Not a teenager or a kid or a promising student, nor a daughter to two devoted parents.

She saw no one, a shadow, a blur. Someone she no longer recognised.

She'd evolved. Into what, she still wasn't sure yet.

Only time would reveal the answer.

A day ago, time delivered. Dani ran her fingertips gently down her stomach, across her waist, up between her breasts and over her shoulder. Sinewy muscle, every inch of her golden body was like granite. She touched the scar on her waist, a thin pale line of damaged skin. For months, that very scar had burned with anger, itched with vehemence. She gazed in the mirror, looked at her Chelsea grin and ran the plan through her head one more time.

Preparation is everything.

A burning raged within her, her mind focused and clear. She stepped to the bed and collected the list.

Reading the names, a crooked smile full of malice crossed her lips.

She was ready.

# THIRTEEN

"You're a fucking dickhead."

"I'm telling you, that chick is giving you the eye. Go over and say hello."

"*Fuck you*," Corey Cross yelled as he necked a shot of tequila and licked the salt covered rim of the glass. His face screwed into a grimace. His hazy, alcohol tainted eyes searched the darkened room for the mystery woman his colleague was alluding to. The strobe lights flashing in time to the thumping techno music weren't helping his cause.

Alan Cahill gulped a quarter of a pint of beer and wiped his lips, stroking his ragged moustache with his sleeve. He pointed across the room, roughly in the direction of the woman, his alcohol fuelled confidence affecting his motor functions. He leaned in close to Corey. "I'm telling you, the chick in the leather coat with the dyke haircut is giving you the eye. I want you to go over there and take her home. I'll give you twenty bucks if you *fuck* her."

Corey downed another shot of tequila. "Twenty? Try thirty."

Alan nodded. "Done."

Corey climbed off his stool, staggered and balanced himself on the bar. Using his left hand, he slicked his hair back onto his greasy head and put on his best smile.

The effect was two scrunched lips forming a crooked grin, which only emphasised his yellowing teeth rimmed with plaque, his gums receding from the poor hygiene. He straightened his clothing, hoisting his loose jeans to his waist, ambled across the room, head bobbing to the music, and finally set his eyes on the woman.

"Hi," he said.


Dani knew Corey was going to approach before she sat down. She was wearing a tight leather jacket with a white t-shirt that stretched tightly across her toned form, riding just above her belly button. The starkness of the shirt enhanced her tan and perfectly accompanied her belly button ring, a double diamond that hung provocatively. Her blue jeans, Dani's preferred attire, created curves in all the right places. As she sipped her orange juice through a pink straw, she eyed her foes at the bar. She tugged on the short, blonde wig that hid her long, brown locks. It held firm.

*Is the makeup good enough?*

*It will be.*

*You've never tried it before.*

*The scars aren't visible in broad daylight with it; you'll be fine in here.*

Dani closed her eyes and composed herself. *Besides, they'll be too drunk to notice.*

Her stare was piercing and seductive enough to catch their attention. They took the bait as men do…easily. When Alan looked too, confirming both of their attentions, she flicked them a coy smile, making sure she licked the tip of the straw.

*Bingo.*

*See! It worked.*

Dani surveyed the room.

Multiple people of all ages and genders were partying the night away, erasing their daily woes born from work and marriage and poor finances. Some performed with youthful abandon, many danced timidly, hands close, heads down.

One or two were harassing strangers, asking them to dance or trying to impress them. One man was strutting his stuff, thrusting towards a female rump only hidden by a tight mini skirt and dark shadow.

Dani never got to experience a proper Friday night, a night out on the town with her friends. That 'luxury' was ripped from her life. On observation, as her unimpressed eye roamed the room and it's shameless, oblivious occupants, she wasn't missing much. She remembered tasting vodka once and retched, spitting it out. That, combined with the loud music, the heavy bass already inducing a throbbing migraine in her skull, convinced her she'd missed absolutely nothing.

No, she was fine as she was.

She averted her gaze to her targets.

*Show time.*

After a moment, Corey stumbled over, acting cool and confident, an intoxicated swagger nipping at his walk, his legs nearly giving way. He took a few seconds to adjust himself in front of Dani. "Hi."

"Hi," Dani smiled, leaning her chin down slightly to sip her drink, ensuring her glittery lips and radiant eyes did the work. Corey groaned; his fluctuating gaze not subtle about his ambitions. Dani felt sick inside, and squirmed a little at the perverted stare, but continued.

*Not long now, just play dumb.*

"What's your name?"

"Corey."

"Cool name. Like the singer of that band?"

"Huh?"

Dani rolled her eyes. "Never mind. Where's your friend?"

"Oh, he's going home to his wife."

Corey snorted as if telling the funniest joke he'd ever heard.

Dani smiled, humouring him. "Shame."

"Shame? *Baby*, I'm more man than you'll *ever* need."

"I'd like to see that."

Dani stood up and stepped in close to Corey. "I hope I can handle you…" She glanced down at his groin and turned away.

"Where you goin'?"

"I'm a two man woman. No friend, no play."

"What? You want us *both*?"

"Yes…why? Got a problem with that, *Corey*?"

Corey's alcohol slurred mind did the math in about three seconds, but took about thirty seconds to comprehend. He gulped, the blurring image of the attractive woman before him swirling erratically. His brain kicked into gear, the fear of losing his conquest dictating everything.

He had to find Alan.

*No friend - no fucky fucky.*

*Insane!*

"Wait here, I'll be right back."

Corey stumbled away to find his friend. As he did, the smile vanished from Dani's face and she opened her purse. Checking she had everything required, she closed it and waited.

*Just a few hours more. Get them drunk.*

*Then, the fun begins.*


"This alley here will be fine…we can't go home…the wife won't appreciate it."

Alan, who was leading the way, staggered into the dimly lit alleyway behind the bar. He stumbled against an empty dumpster, a piercing clang echoing down the narrow street as he shouldered into it. Corey followed slowly; his hand wrapped loosely around Dani's. As all three emerged in the vast, dark space between the buildings, Corey let go of Dani's hand and put his arms in the air, punching it with drunken happiness.

"*Wooo!*"

He joined his friend and they hugged, ardently slapping one another on the back. Dani didn't smile.

It didn't matter; the low light hid the scorn that darkened her face. She edged towards the slimy, piss-stained wall, lurking in the shadows, keeping her distance. Now, the mood was joyous and innocent, but Dani expected it to change at any second.

It didn't take long.

Corey spun around, his left foot dragging in a puddle of yellow liquid. "Now…Sarah…that's your name, isn't it? I want you to fuck me first…it'll benefit me financially I have some serious moolah riding on it –"

"– you fucktard, its thirty measly quid," Alan quipped.

"Whatever! I'm getting paid to *fuck*. That makes me a whore…wait…" He prodded the tips of his fingers, then laughed, the logic disappearing on a warm, fruity belch. He pointed at Alan, who laughed merrily. "You challenged me, I get dibs. Besides, I don't want your sloppy seconds.

Alan shrugged, his eyes flickering closed for a second.

Corey continued. "Then, I want you to suck his cock…and then he'll fuck you in the arse. He's married, he can't fuck cunt…but everything else is okay." Alan chuckled. Corey attempted a high five with his friend and completely missed in his drunken stupor, slipping comically to the ground.

Alan shuffled to his feet and did a little dance. "The wife will never know…"

Corey rolled around on the soaked ground. "Make sure you wipe the shit off your bell end though…I heard that happened to Jeff. His wife could smell the curry from his hooker's back door. She surprised him on his return home, dropped to her knees, and got a curried mouthful. It coated the inside of his foreskin and, in turn, her mouth." He stumbled to his feet, leaning on the battered brick wall beside him. "She nearly rumbled our organisation. Apparently, she went up and down the streets, looking for the whore responsible. Rhodes ordered Jeff to kill her for that; it was too close to home. Tragic really, Jeff's wife was a fitty."

Dani remained stoic; a sense of achievement arose inside at the mention of Rhodes' name. She was definitely on the right track. Dani made a mental note of Rhodes' activities, cataloguing the details from the inebriated conversation.

"Man, that's fucking sick. Jeff should have known better though. You don't fuck with Rhodes. His wife found out the hard way."

"Yeah, you don't *fuck* with the merchandise. And you don't fuck it either."

Corey and Alan erupted in a fit of laughter, neither paying attention to Dani, who remained silent.

The two men patted each other on the chest repeatedly, balancing on one another, and stumbled towards her. Corey started to unbuckle his belt. Alan placed a hand on his friend's chest. "Whoa, whoa, I just thought. If we have a three way, make sure you keep your dick away from me. I ain't queer."

"What?" Corey uttered, realising the implications. His eyes widened. "You do the same; I don't want you in me or on me or even getting your spunk on me. Gross."

"So we're clear…we only fuck 'er," Alan aimed his wobbling thumb at Dani and missed completely.

Corey nodded silently.

Alan's glassy eyes pierced through Dani, sending a shiver up her spine.

"Time for some fun," Corey spluttered. "Come sit on my cock."

Dani stepped forward. "What if I say no?"

"Then that's called being a prick tease. Do it," replied Corey.

"You can't bring us out here and not fuck us…," Alan didn't finish his sentence, losing his train of thought. After a second, he continued. "Yeah…"

"What if I changed my mind?" Dani decided to test the waters. *If she was going to do some damage, might as well have a good fucking reason*, she thought. She looked at Corey, loading the question to him.

"You don't get to change your mind, Sarah. This isn't a fucking bake sale."

"Some people call that rape," Dani said, her voice controlled.

Corey grinned. "Rape…a funny word that. Yes, no, who cares. I'm fucking you whether you like it or not. Get your jeans off. I bet that pussy is wet and tight."

Corey lowered his trousers, working his semi-erect penis beneath his briefs. The trousers dropped and the belt buckle clanged loudly on the wet ground below. Several coins spilled from the pockets and rolled into a puddle of urine by the wall. In the background, Alan was tensing up.

Dani stepped forward once more.

Corey smiled. "Feeling a bit groggy are we?"

"How do you mean?"

"My friend slipped some pills into your drink…you know, to get the *mood* going."

"Did he now? Does he know that's illegal?" Dani placed a hand to her forehead.

"The law doesn't apply to us, lady. People like us are untouchable. We had a feeling you might change your mind; whores do that on occasion. We don't take chances."

"But I thought you were the whore? You're the one getting paid," Dani uttered, sidestepping from the shadows.

Corey smiled. "Oh, yeah. That's true. However, that's a technicality. You're the real *whore* in this situation. You want to fuck two cocks. And I *ain't* changing my mind."

"So we're agreed, you're the whore?"

"Yeah, so?"

"Does that mean drugs don't work on you?"

"Huh?"

"You're not the only person who spiked a drink tonight."

Almost on cue, Alan toppled to the wet ground, smacking his head on the wet concrete, his face landing in a puddle of piss. Corey turned around, the smile vanishing from his face. "Alan? Get up you dumb shit."

Dani took her opportunity and stepped forward. "And I didn't drink mine." Corey spun to face the woman. "What the…?"

The bowie knife in Dani's hand shot up and sliced into Corey's penis. The blade spliced the erect member, the tip ripping through the engorged shaft and emerging through the skin and muscle on the top side with a sick, soggy punch. Corey gasped, overwhelming pain crippling his body, the wind ripped from his lungs, instantly reducing him to a gibbering wreck.

Dani gripped the knife and moved it back and forth, tearing the skin and muscle even more. Blood dribbled and sluiced to the ground with frequent, heavy splats. A low whine slipped from Corey's lips, his face pale with pain and his body shivering with shock. His eyes began to roll into the back of his head.

"Try fucking me now, cunt." Dani removed the blade. Blood gushed from the wound, spraying Corey's legs and Dani's boots. Dani stepped back, watching him bleed out. He wouldn't survive the night. Dani stepped to a puddle, paused, and dipped her boots in them, washing the blood off. Corey, a mumbling, shaking wreck, curled into a ball. Dani felt a hint of a smile on her face. It tugged at the scar lines, which prompted her to stop.

She turned to the unconscious Alan, who was spread-eagled on the floor.

"What are we going to do with you?" Dani whispered to herself.

*She had some ideas.* The smile returned this time. It didn't leave her face.

# FOURTEEN

Dani sipped her coffee and waited.

The hot, bitter liquid tingled on her interior cheek scars, a feeling that subsided with every lush mouthful. She remembered the first time she'd drank coffee, six weeks after major facial surgery, and how she'd yelped at the flash of pain, the black drink spilling over her pale chin. Luckily it had been hospital issued, so it was lukewarm and no serious injury occurred, but from that day forward Dani had been cautious with her hot beverages. Her mother never let her drink the stuff, probably for the same reasons her brother couldn't consume fizzy drinks, so when she'd discovered it, coffee became the first real thing she could call hers, the first exciting discovery of her adult life.

A year ago. She remembered the moment as if it occurred yesterday.

She thought back to Teddy and her mother, bickering over the slightest little thing, over too many video games, and the consumption of cola and bread before dinner. Remembered how the memory stung of a loving fondness, a prickly adoration, one that warmed her heart and, a year ago, would have reduced her to tears.

That was before.

This is now.

Teddy's face slammed into her consciousness, heavy and colossal, like a high-resolution photograph thrust in her face. She gasped, surprised, shocked at the clarity of the vivid visage. She saw her brother chuckle, his cheeks rosy with exertion as he toppled off the second stair onto the new carpet, cursing as he got his pyjama legs tangled beneath his feet. She could hear his innocent voice, smell the Imperial Leather soap that he denied loving, but secretly could not live without. Every evening, after dinner, he would wash his chubby hands with it, in the upstairs bathroom. She'd caught him sniffing them on more than one occasion, in secret, her brother oblivious to his big sister prying and spying. Until, one fateful evening, he'd turned around.

She remembered laughing and pointing, and he responded in his normal way. "Don't you tell anyone, *you cow, you...dobber boffin face!"*

*Dobber boffin face.*

She blinked and the memory of her brother dissipated, pushed to a dark recess of her brain. For the first time in months, a tear slowly rolled down her cheek.

She slapped it away, furious.

*Damn it, tears are for the weak.*

*You're just tired.*

*Or, it's because you have one of them, him, right there, in front of you.*

*You can finally do something; you can start to seek vengeance. For Teddy. For Mum. This is the plan, coming to fruition. An extensive, detailed, well-laid plan that's about to kick-start into action.*

She looked at her paper cup, shook it, and narrowed her eyes. Dani glanced at the dishevelled wig on the table, a short spiky hairdo purchased from a small store in Soho, the one she'd used to fool Corey and Alan. Using the bottom of her cup, she brushed it gently.

Slight movement ahead averted her attention.

She checked her watch slowly. *Seven hours. Impressive.*

Dani ran her hands through her scraggly hair and down to her shoulders, interlacing her fingers at the back of her neck and flexed, pushing on her spine, stretching away the tiredness from her torso. She ached and creaked in places, but she had work to do. She gulped the remainder of her cold coffee and sighed.

*Yeah, carrying the fucker from the car hadn't helped. Dead weight.*

Dani stood up, pushing her chair aside, and strolled over to her motionless captive. She kept her distance; walked slowly, observing, ensuring she didn't move too fast. Sure, she was tired, but rushing wouldn't solve a thing, the situation needed to play out normally.

She imagined a voice-over in a movie saying those exacts words and shook her head.

Dani stopped several metres short, stood still and watched.

She'd strapped Alan to a metal chair. His zip-tied hands looped beneath his seat, unmovable, restricted by the steel legs pinning them in place. His feet were flat, his ankles tied tight to the chair legs. His chin was low, not quite touching his chest, which expanded shallowly, slowly. The breathing was controlled and rhythmic; he wasn't quite awake yet.

Dani leant down and pulled a folding stool from the wall. She opened it and placed it a few feet before her captive. She didn't sit. She merely stood watching, waiting.

She waited five minutes before Alan moved again.

This time, his eyes opened.

"Urghhhh…" Alan rolled sideways in his chair, his equilibrium catatonic. His eyes darted left and right, squinting, offended by the bright light that suddenly ambushed them. He tried to squirm away but couldn't, his hands bound, his feet tied equally tight. He flopped about in the chair and finally came to a rest. Dani noticed a sheen of sweat and urine on his face, an exclamation of confusion and pain screwing his features into a hideous grimace.

Dani unfolded her arms and cracked her knuckles. The sound was loud, almost ear splitting in the silent, abandoned warehouse.

Alan heard it, flinched, and looked up.

He groaned.

Then, his eyes widened. "*You.*"

Dani said nothing. She simply remained where she was, her steely eyes boring into her foe. She was aware of the shadow that shrouded her, provided her some respite from the light that was shining directly on Alan. She knew he couldn't see her face, not yet anyway.

But, he recognised her leather jacket regardless. That saved her some time.

"Where's Corey?"

Again, Dani remained silent. She took a step left, her feet clonking loudly on the dull, concrete ground. Alan followed her, his eyes pinned on the mysterious woman before him. Dani resumed her vigil once again.

Alan laughed.

He looked down, stringy sputum oozing from his mouth, a side effect of the flunitrazepam currently crippling his motor functions. It smeared his shirt, staining the grey material and darkening it. He looked up again. "What do you want, *bitch*?"

Dani said nothing.

Alan grimaced, his tongue lapping at the excess fluid on his lips. He whipped his head sideways in a useless attempt to push the drool to his darting, probing tongue. In another life, Dani might have found this amusing, since he'd face planted into a puddle of urine only a few hours previously.

Her face remained stoic.

Alan laughed again, weaker this time. "So, that was your plan? Attack us and take us hostage? I have to give it to you, lady, you have a pair of fuckin' balls on you." He spat a phlegmy wad on the floor, expelling the sputum from his system. "You have a pair of fuckin' balls, but fuckin' shit for brains. Do you know who we *are*?"

Again, Dani said nothing, but she was expecting this line of questioning. The bravado, the testosterone-fuelled mantra of any male who belonged to a group of gangsters or hoodlums.

She took a small step forward, closing the distance between them slowly.

A statement, an indication that she didn't fear Alan or his company. Fearless.

Alan knew it. He sat up straight, licking his soggy lips, re-evaluating the situation. He knew the woman in the shadows was that hot, dyke-looking chick from the bar, the one with the tight arse, the spiky hair and the quirky, lopsided smile.

*She doesn't have a spiky hairdo now, that's obvious by the shadow.*

*Maybe it's someone else.*

*Maybe it was a wig? Women love that shit.*

*What was her name? Sarah? That's it.*

*Why won't she say something?* He rolled his tongue in his mouth and breathed deep, preparing himself.

Before he could say anything, Dani took another step forward.

Alan's eyes widened. "I…I wouldn't do that if I were you."

"And why is that?" Dani replied, keeping her voice low, calm. She felt an anger coursing through her veins, one that threatened to propel her to sadistic violence. Her blood boiled, she listened to her fingers clenching and unclenching, her tendons creaking as she eased the stress from every inch of her toned body. Her face burned, the puffy scar marks itching something fierce. She wondered if she could do any damage by shouting, something she hadn't done since the night of the attack.

This man…this man worked with her father, he's an employee of the organisation who sanctioned his execution, takes a pay packet from the sadistic fuck who ordered the death of an innocent family. She realised she was feeling nauseous, the acrid taste singed the back of her throat; sick, anger and good will stirred an unbalanced pit of despair in her stomach. Dani closed her eyes and counted to ten.

One…

*You should have prepared for this, should have planned for this eventuality.*

Two…

*If he sees you, feels you're breaking, this is all for nothing.*

Three…

*Calm down. You're so close. You can do this.*

On four, Alan interrupted her.

"Look at you. What a fuckin' bottler. Look at you standing there in the shadows, scared to approach me. Me, Alan Cahill." Alan spat again, his face burning red with vehemence. "Do you know who I *fuckin'* am? I'm a *fuckin' God* amongst men and women; I work for the toughest cunt in London. I work for Ross Rhodes, that's *fuckin' right*. All Rhodes lead to death, that's him. If he gets a whiff of this shit, he'll be down here like a fuckin' shot. He'll raze your pathetic life, your inbred family, and your fuckin' existence to the fuckin' ground. Now, *let me go!*"

Dani opened her eyes, the silence returning on the back of Alan's tirade.

Suddenly, Dani felt calm. All was fine.

"Look at you, you cunt! What you gonna…"

Dani stepped out of the shadows and walked over to Alan, her stride filled with purpose. Without stopping, she closed a sinewy fist and smashed Alan in the cheek. The impact cracked in the air with a soggy splat – blood and sputum whipped away and pattered the concrete. Alan groaned, his mouth dribbling pink into his lap. Dani unclenched her hand, feeling the throbbing there. She knew it would bruise; it was inevitable. She could feel the muscle contracting already.

Alan laughed. "That's more like it…you got some fuckin' spunk in you. Balls and spunk, who'd have thunk it. You have plenty…for a whore that is."

Dani sidled to the left and launched her head forward, cracking Alan's nose with her forehead. Her skull rang as she connected, bouncing her brain, the impact momentarily blasting stars and bright lights through her 20/20 vision.

Dani backed off and turned away, rubbing her throbbing forehead.

"Arghhh…uh…you bitch, you…you boke my nose. Fud you…you boke my nose."

Dani ran her fingertips across her face, testing the scars. Nothing wet secreted from them. She felt the inside of both cheeks with her tongue, tasting for blood. There was none. The head butt had been unintentional, a spur of the moment reaction to a man who was quickly fraying her patience. It caught her off guard; she hadn't expected such a reaction. For the last year, she'd disciplined herself, taught herself to remain emotionless and cold during moments like this.

Except she'd never had any *real* moments to practice with.

*A big flaw*, she thought.

However, she felt alive, ignited.

A warm sensation boiled within her, one that tickled her face with a laugh, one that threatened to push her into giddiness. She turned back to Alan and licked her upper lip. She used the back of her hand to wipe her forehead, which shone with sweat. She tucked her hair behind her head.

*Time to go to work.*

Alan snorted, blowing pink snot and blood onto his lap. "Shit…shit," he exclaimed. He looked up, his eyes falling on the long hair, the pale scar tissue.

"Hey, you…you aren't der…her?" His eyes widened in absolute horror. "Oh, *fuck*…no, it can't…it…*you*!"

Dani said nothing, her eyes narrowing.

"It can't be…you're dead, *dead!* Brad…he…*he killed you.* No one could survive dat." Alan fell silent, running some terrifying thoughts through his head. Blood trickled from his shattered nose, coating his facial hair in crimson. His eyes widened again. "I'm sorry, I didn't mean to day what I bid, you know, about your family and tuff." He cleared his throat. "That was stupid of me."

Dani ambled over to Alan. "Rhodes. Where is he?"

Alan shook his head, snorting blood and clogging snot into his lap; a disbelieving smile hitched his cheeks high, his yellow teeth exposed, specked with red.

He winced when his nose pounded his brain with white agony. "I can't…can't tell you that."

"You can and you will."

Dani leaned in close, ensuring Alan could see the scar tissue, the ragged wounds that twisted her once pretty face into a permanent grin. "You can and you will, and there is no optional answer for this one."

"But…he'd kill me."

"You're going to die either way," Dani said flatly.

Alan laughed. "No, you…you wouldn't?"

Dani nodded.

"I would. Luckily, for the female population of London, tonight, you ran into me. Sure, you tried to spike my drink and rape me and gangbang me with your friend, Corey. I even said no and you insisted. That makes you a rapist, and in my eyes, all rapists should face their punishment."

Alan sniffed. "Rapists don't face the death sentence here…"

"You seem to be confusing me with the law. I'm not the law. If I were, I'd be failing the innocent right now, convicting the wrong person or letting a rapist walk free. No, I'm something more lethal, more…productive." Dani straightened up and circled Alan. "Your boss ordered a hit on my father. In the process, he killed my little brother and my mother. He nearly killed me."

"We heard the dory."

His shattered nose was still affecting his speech. "Brad…he bragged about dit, dold us everything."

Dani felt her heart lurch and she nearly gagged. She stood behind Alan, tempted to break his neck and end it right there. She needed information though, information only he could provide.

"So, Bradley bragged, huh? I thought he would. The guy had a boner the entire time he was…mutilating me. He did this to my face; did he tell you that? He cut into my teenage face with a pair of kitchen scissors as if I was a piece of fucking chicken. He kicked me around like a football and nearly broke my neck."

Alan nodded. "Yep."

"So, tell me, Alan. Do you think he should be walking free," Dani said, pointing behind her, "walking around and living his life? Inflicting pain on others? Do you think I deserved to have my life torn from me, my family butchered in front of me?"

Alan laughed, clearing his throat. "Bitch, you're going to kill me anyway, why should I side with you? Your father, Dennis, was a fuckin' liability. Bradley? He's a sound guy, the best executioner I ever saw. I'm glad he's on our side. You? You're nothing to me. I hope you fucking suffered."

"Best executioner? If he's such a good executioner, how comes I'm still alive?"

Alan didn't have a response for that.

Dani snorted.

"I'm alive because he let me live. He was going to kill me, would have probably blown my head off, just like my little brother…did he tell you that bit? How he shot an eight-year-old boy in the head with a pump action?"

Alan shook his head slowly, concern registering on his face.

"He shot my brother and let me live. He let me live because, funny thing this, he wanted me to find him, hunt him down, challenge him. I never thought he'd take me up on it, but he did. I talked a lot of shit when my life was in danger, but your executioner – the man you so loyally worship – he let me go. That's how I survived, because of chauvinistic male bravado. He wanted a challenge from a seventeen-year-old girl."

Alan sniffed, snot and blood dribbling down his broken, sweaty face. "Bullshib. He always dinishes the job."

Dani leant down behind Alan and pulled the strings on a black bag. Gently, she placed a hand inside and lifted an object out. She stood up and walked before Alan, dropping the object in his lap with a soggy squelch.

Alan screamed at the bloody phallic object that rolled around in his lap. The penis, split unevenly down the middle, leaving the edges ragged and raw, was still connected to the testicles, their shriveled sacks encrusted in mucus and blood.

Alan buckled; vomit spewing from between his quivering lips, splattering his legs, wracking his body so severely that he nearly toppled backwards. "You *fucking bitch*, you're *fucking crazy*!"

Dani placed a foot on his seat, between his flailing legs, and brought him back level. She placed her bloody fingers on Alan's face and wiped Corey's blood down his cheeks, dotting his slick forehead with her fingertips. The muted hiss of a releasing bladder filled the air, the piss washing the blood from the front of Alan's trousers; the combined mess dribbling to the concrete.

Dani stared into his eyes. "Bradley let me live, and because of that, a whole chain of events happened. I located you and your friends, all too easily, ran into you and seduced you in a bar. After we left, I drugged you and castrated Corey. I cut his genitals off slowly and gently with a bowie knife. Then, I put them in a velvet bag, brought you to a warehouse that, frankly, was too easy to lease, and tied you up."

Dani glanced around and shook her head in disbelief.

"We've been here for *seven* hours and I haven't heard a peep from anyone outside. No one knows we're here and no one gives a flying fuck. It's too *easy*; you should be more secure, more alert, especially if Rhodes' organisation is as perfect as you make it out. Instead, you're tied to a chair with piss in your little boy's pants and your friends cock in your lap. Now, you *are* going to die, slowly, surely, and you will tell me everything I want to know beforehand. You know how I know this?"

Alan shook his head; his eyes pinned on the gore in his soggy lap. "You're…you're fuckin' *crazy*."

"I know this because I have nothing to lose. You will tell me everything, even if I have to yank your fingernails off with a pair of pliers, twist your scrotum around the blade of a kitchen knife or, my favourite, if I have to dismantle your body piece by bloody piece with a meat cleaver and mail it back to your friends. Then, I will find your wife and do the same to her. And her family. You take mine, I'll take yours. I won't stop until they break your fucking code and let me know where Ross Rhodes is."

Alan smiled as his sanity slipped, his teeth shining bright pink with blood. "I knew there was a woman like you somewhere. And you know what? I've had enough. You're gonna kill me anyway, so why should I tell you shit? You ain't getting a fucking thing out of me. Do your worst."

Dani smiled. She felt the grin tugging on her scars and this time, she didn't care. It highlighted her expression, created a macabre image of horror on her mutilated face. She walked over to the table and tossed her coffee cup aside, scooping up a heavy black bag. She turned and walked back to Alan slowly, the bag clinking as she did. She dropped it to the floor with a metallic thud.

"Last chance?"

"Fuck you, *whore*. Good luck in finding Rhodes."

Dani nodded. "Just remember, this is happening because of Bradley. This is his fault. Remember that. Unlike me, though, you're not going to survive this."

# FIFTEEN

"Where are those fucking clowns?"

Bradley ran his fingertips along his eyebrows, his brow furrowing at the sound of his companion's voice. He sighed deeply, the deserted road beyond the rain-spattered windshield beginning to bore him. The rain had let up, reduced to the occasional dull thud as a stray drop from the overhead power cables hit the soaked bonnet of the vehicle.

"They're two hours late."

He fumbled in his pocket and retrieved his Zippo.

Bradley stared at it, admired the craftsmanship, enamored as the moonlight danced off the stainless steel and its precise engravings. He flicked the lighter lid open, ignited it, stared at the dancing yellow flame and closed it.

He repeated the process.

Once, twice, three times.

"Do you mind?" Philip Andrews uttered, his eyes staring at a particular street, one he expected his companions to emerge from at any second. The more he stared, the more frustrated he became. He concentrated, blurring everything around the dark street until it was his primary, and only, focus.

He felt his anger rise – every second with no result made him seethe more, his patience fraying. "*Fuck!*" His left hand opened in the air, signaling his frustration.

Bradley smiled. "They're not coming," he said, his voice gravelly and low. "These guys are clowns, but they're never late."

"Well, I hate to disappoint you, but they *are* late…see?" Andrews tapped his Rolex with a sturdy fingertip.

Bradley felt his jaw knotting. Andrews was a mouthy shit and always had to have the last word, much like his 'companions,' Corey and Alan. When the three of them were together, they resembled a living, walking frat house; the rich kids that make university a living hell for the normal, self-funded students. Money went into everything, and there was no expense spared. They had to drink the best champagne, dine in the most luxurious restaurants, normally to impress or attract a pretty female in the same room – which was Rhodes' fault really for paying them too much, but they did a good job. Idiots, yes, but useful and loyal.

Still, when the company prides itself on keeping a low profile, one of the key reasons for their success, having those jokers on the payroll always threatened to come back and bite them in the arse.

It hadn't…yet.

Still, it didn't make him like them any more than his job required. He shot a sideways glance at Andrews and chuckled.

Andrews noticed. "What's so funny?"

"Oh nothing. Just find it amusing how stress doesn't agree with you."

"Stressed? Why shouldn't I be? These guys are late, fucking *late*! In this business, that usually means one of two things."

"What you think they jumped ship? Went to the competition? I think you overestimate their mental capacity somewhat."

Andrews shook his head. "I didn't say that. I was thinking the other thing."

Bradley didn't reply to that, and turned back to the windscreen. He didn't like Corey or Alan, but the thought of them dead in an alley somewhere did unnerve him slightly. Recruitment was a bitch.

"You tried calling them?" Bradley said, tucking his lighter away.

"Several times. No answer."

"Where were they last?"

"They said they were hitting a bar in town...Sin or something...I don't know, some cheap, sticky club that attracts a horrible crowd."

"Cheap? You guys don't do cheap."

"Yeah well, it's pay day on Friday. So sue me."

"Really? You guys are *that* haphazard with your cash?"

"Fuck you."

Bradley laughed. "Well, luckily I know the club you mean. It's 2am. Would they still be there?"

"Only one way to find out," Andrews spat.

Bradley nodded, turning the key in the ignition. "Lucky me."


*****


The water sluiced down the drain, a dark crimson vortex of violence and pain and suffering.

Dani sighed deeply, her arms burning, the muscles tense from an evening's workout. She pressed her palms against the slippery wall and gazed down, flexing and groaning, breathing out slowly, exhaling the hurt from her system. She lifted her left leg high, bending it at the knee, rising it towards her chest slowly. She placed it down and repeated the process with her right leg. Once done, she faced down again, the stream of water drenching the back of her taut neck.

Her balance didn't waver once.

She glanced up and screamed into the spray, spurting the water off to the left.

Then, for the first time in a year, she cried.

The spray from the showerhead cleansed the salty tears away, caressing her hot cheeks, the torrents exploded off her blood-soaked body in a cacophony of splashing. Her cheeks stung, the reformed tissue felt sore and puffy, but she didn't care.

She stood like that until the water ran cold.

She didn't keep track of the time.

\*\*\*\*\*

"The place is closed."

Bradley drummed his fingers on the greasy roof, the car humming slothfully below his crossed arms. The chaos of a Friday night unravelled around him like a macabre, badly written play. He saw one thing: A society disrupted by alcohol, drugs and merriment, who went about their business without a care or shred of self-respect in the world.

He searched the rain-spattered pavement, amused and disgusted in equal measure. The streetlights glared off the slick concrete, providing a distorted, illuminated runway to the proceedings.

A group of women, clearly inebriated, were staggering and fighting with their balance, leaning on one another for support. The prettiest of the bunch, carrying an empty champagne bottle, and whose mascara streaked across her attractive face, collapsed in the gutter. Her legs splayed as she hit the deck, her crumpled white panties – and her modesty – on display to the world. Her friends howled in laughter, pointing at their fallen comrade, sniggering and slapping one another playfully.

One of them noticed Bradley's disgusted gaze, sneered and flipped him the bird. "Take a fuckin' picture, you filthy pervert, it'll last longer!"

Bradley laughed and ignored them.

On the other side of the street, between an abandoned estate agents and a bustling kebab shop, a group of teenage boys were hassling a homeless man, pulling at his withered blanket and throwing litter into his grubby domain.

The man had his gloved hands over his head, cowering away, cold and frightened. One boy stepped out of the kebab shop and poured a portion of chips over his head, mocking him. His friend, who proceeded to urinate on the wall beside the defenseless man, gave his friend a swerving high five that missed.

Andrews stepped into Bradley's line of view. "Did you hear me? Place is closed!"

"I heard you," Bradley said under his breath. Behind his vehicle, a taxi driver was tossing a man out onto the curb, his pink designer shirt smeared in lumpy vomit. The stench reached Bradley, who crinkled his nose. "People make me fucking sick."

"Oi, *wanker!*"

Bradley turned around. A girl with tussled black hair and a sweaty complexion stood before him. Her mascara was still intact but her lipstick shade left a lot to be desired. Her cheeks sparkled with glitter, the shine dulled by excessive orange foundation. She was shorter and plumper then her friends, and reeked of cigarettes and alcohol, but in a normal setting, without a bucket of makeup, Bradley could imagine her as an attractive young woman. Lack of self-confidence, probably spurred by the presence of her glamorous, idiotic friends, drove her to improve herself, something that would never naturally occur. Makeup and mindless nights on the lash were her solution, probably finished with a rotting kebab and a cry into her pillow. An endless circle.

He wondered if she would ever find herself.

"Oi, wanker!" She laughed and turned to the other women, who weren't paying any attention to their friend's bravado. "You see this, girls? He's ogling my *tits*!"

Bradley smiled. "Can I help you?"

"Yeah, I saw you eyeing up Mercedes over there, you fuckin' pervert. Keep yo fuckin' eyes off, yeah?"

Bradley laughed. "You think I was eyeing up…that," he said, pointing to her friend, who still lay drunk on the pavement. "If you think that, *darling*, you're sorely mistaken."

"Whoa, I ain't your fuckin' darlin,' you got that? Not even in your….dreams, yeah? Just keep your prying eyes off her snatch, okay?"

Bradley shook his head, pinching his nose as he did so.

*An attractive woman, but a dumb one. Uneducated.*

"You listening to me, bruv?"

Bradley sighed. "Loser says what?"

"Wha!"

Bradley punched the woman in the side of the head. She dropped like a rock, cascading into the side of his car with an enormous crash. Her lifeless body hit the wet concrete with a splat. Her purse opened and spilled its contents into the road. Bradley watched as several condoms, lipsticks, drink coupons and tampons fell into the gutter, slowly floating away on the stream of trickling drain water. Much like her friend, her legs spread wide and exposed her naked sex to the entire street. Andrews simply grunted from his side of the car. "Taking out the white trash, I see."

Bradley laughed, genuinely surprised at the humour. He pushed the woman aside with the pointed end of a sleek, leather loafer. "This one neglected to wear panties. Tempted?"

"Fuck that…I mean no, not at all."

Laughing, both men climbed back into the car. Bradley watched the group of women as he turned on the ignition. None of them had noticed their fallen friend.

*Big shock*, he thought. *The runt of the litter…or the clique as it may be.*

"Where to now?"

Bradley grunted. "Rhodes. He needs to know."

At 2:13 am, the evening was just getting started.


\*\*\*\*\*

The bourbon scorched Dani's throat and she retched, gagging, covering her mouth with the back of her hand. She dribbled the remaining liquid back into the glass and placed it on the kitchen counter. She paused, took her cup of coffee, nodded, and moved through the apartment. She closed the bedroom door and sat on the edge of the soft mattress, sipping the hot beverage slowly. The bitterness didn't expel the burning amber in her throat, but it started to replace the horrible taste in her mouth.

Dani placed her coffee on the bedside cabinet and breathed out deeply. She stared down at her hands, fresh and pink and wrinkled from the shower. She saw nothing but blood; oozing, seeping, dripping blood, running up and down her arms in trickling rivulets at triple speed, like a sped up video or a horrific horror movie montage. The droplets spread and flayed, covering every inch of her clean skin, splattering and sluicing to the floor below.

She blinked and the blood was gone, replaced by clean flesh and a sweet confectionary smell. And the bitter essence of coffee, one that soothed and relaxed her. Her mind began to calm, to rationalise her actions from that evening.

It had taken four minutes to get the information she required from Alan.

Alan hadn't cracked, no, he'd remained loyal to his boss. In fairness, Dani hadn't gone very far when his mobile phone rang, shrill and distinct, buzzing in his pocket. She'd applied some lye to his trembling fingertips when one of his work colleagues called, no doubt seeking his presence. He was screaming in pain as the chemical corroded the outer layer of flesh, eating at the second layer within moments.

That's when she realised she didn't need to torture him.

She could take his details, his mobile phone, a mass of data, and use it to her advantage. Much easier.

*Ah, the digital age.*

She took the phone, swiped into the phonebook and found personal and mobile numbers for Rhode's entire organisation. She had addresses, emails and bank details.

Including Bradley. Including Ross.

Jackpot.

She'd poured a bottle of distilled vinegar on the chemical, neutralizing the burns somewhat. Alan groaned, thanking her, happy to keep what was left of his fingertips. He thanked her repeatedly, pleading with her for his freedom.

Then, she'd shot him in the face.

The gunshot was loud, alarming, and it made Dani jump. She'd practiced at a gun range with the weapon – in a small corner of London with a fake license and lack security – but the gun was much louder without ear protection. She jumped; with the gun steady in her hand, she squeezed the trigger and fired a second shot, one that blew off the top of Alan's head, spraying gloopy brain and skull across the concrete. Alarmed and surprised, Dani had recovered, wrapped the corpse in a tarpaulin and ditched it in a rusted bathtub at the back of the warehouse. She didn't clean up, knowing nothing could be traced back to her.

In hindsight, that might have been a stupid thing to do. However, she'd selected the neighbourhood for its heavy criminal activity. Arson, burglary, car theft, muggings, ASBOs. And when the warehouse rental guys had asked for a name, she'd given Mrs Cahill.

A lie. A lie for the sake of murder.

*Murder.*

*What have I done?*

The cool, damp hair on her shoulder reminded her of the shower, her first shower since ending two lives, one used to wash away the blood and horror and memories already embossed on her brain.

She twisted her hair between her nervous fingers, water seeping from the locks and pattering the bed below. The tears had stopped, but the remorse didn't.

Revenge was the plan.

*You're one of them now.*

The words sent a shiver trembling down her spine.

*Yes, she wanted justice for her family, but resorting to murder to achieve it?*

*You should call the police and inform Detective Inspector Scott. They ended the investigation because they were in the dark. You know where Rhodes is, you can ship him to the police.*

*Take him down legally.*

Dani glanced at the bedside cabinet and looked at Scott's crinkled yellow card. She'd put it in the box with her personal belongings. She'd kept it, a reminder that some humanity existed in the world. After all, he'd stayed by her bedside, day and night, the only person who did.

True, he had an agenda, he was doing this job, but he still cared for her wellbeing.

She owed it to him.

She also owed it to Teddy.

And Mum.

And, in some way, despite it being his fault, her Dad too.

Her eyes closed and reopened, this time focusing on Alan's phone, which sat next to the card. It stunk of vomit; the bile had seeped into his pockets and smeared the phone during their little talk. Despite cleaning it, the device emitted a lingering, bitter stench into the air.

She thought back to that night. To her dead mother, to Teddy's head as it exploded in her face, destroying her innocence and her life in one gory second of violence.

She swallowed a hot mouthful of coffee and nodded firmly, her decision made.

She picked up the phone and started scrolling through it. Different folders, email accounts and multiple text messages whizzed by. She found naked pictures and swiftly skipped them, hitting the red trash icon as she did, providing some kind of useless humility service to the foolish women in the images. Besides, Alan wouldn't need them anymore.

She backed out and found the phonebook. She scanned the numbers. Her eyes widened when she settled on one specific entry.

Boss.

She remembered it from earlier. It was all too easy.

She drank another mouthful of coffee and shook her head, breathing deep. Then, she dialled.

*****

"So you're telling me that you can't find these pricks anywhere in London?"

Bradley nodded silently, not making eye contact. Andrews shifted nervously beside him, sweating. Rhodes, sat behind his desk with an empty tumbler in his left hand, was bobbing in his leather chair, thinking.

"London's a big place. I doubt you searched very hard. This is not the type of incompetence I expect from you, Bradley."

Bradley nodded. "With all due respect, sir, I'm not their babysitter. That's Andrews' job." Bradley hiked his thumb towards his associate.

"Hey, fuck you. I don't babysit anyone," Andrews spat, his fear dispersing for a second. Rhodes glared at him, which soon reignited his nervousness.

"They're your responsibility, Andrews. You should know where they are at all times."

Bradley smirked.

Andrews fell silent, wiping his slick forehead.

"Anyway, it doesn't matter. For all we know the dumb cunts are pissed up in a gutter somewhere sniffing coke from a whore's shitty arse crack. If they don't make their presence known by morning, send Sanchez. He'll find them. He always does."

"Sanchez is an assassin, sir," Andrews queried.

"Yes; and when they see him in their vicinity, they will soon fall into line. I might even have him tap one of them with a bullet, for maximum impact."

"Good idea," Bradley uttered. "This is a professional company. Have him shoot them in the dick; it might domesticate them a little."

It was Andrews' turn to smirk – a look that said, *'Way to go, brownnose, and fuck you.'*

"Bradley, I want you to take off, get some rest. Andrews, bunk up in the dorms, we have an early start ahead of us. Sanchez won't appreciate being woken at the crack of dawn."

Andrews shook his head. "I wouldn't worry, sir, I heard he doesn't sleep –"

"– did I ask for your opinion, you daft cunt? It's because of you that they're missing in the first fucking place, I..." Rhodes stopped speaking and stared down at his desk, grinning. "Well, look at that, speak of the fucking devil." Rhodes snatched his mobile phone from the desk and tapped the screen. He glared at Andrews. "Cahill, where the fuck are you?"

A muted, digital hissing filled the room before Bradley and Andrews realised the handset was on speakerphone. They crowded around the desk, watching their boss, listening intently. Rhodes placed the phone gently on the oak surface. No words came through the speaker. "Cahill, can you hear me? If you fucking drunk dialled me, I'm going to personally cut your balls off."

Still nothing, only the long, muted hiss.

*"Cahill!"*

"Is this Ross Rhodes?"

The voice was unfamiliar, stunted, groggy sounding.

It wasn't Cahill. Rhodes looked to Andrews and Bradley, both of whom shrugged. Rhodes looked down again, a grimace appearing on his face. "Who is this?"

"Is this Ross *Rhodes*?"

Rhodes cracked his neck and sighed. "Yeah, who wants to know?"

"Good."

The person cleared their throat, the phlegmy harking distorting the sound. Silence followed for a second and all three men looked at each other, confused. "Good, then I have your attention."

The voice was female, lighter in tone, spiked with a lisp or a speech impediment on every third or fourth word. "Ross Rhodes, I believe you knew my father, Dennis."

Andrews' eyes widened and he looked straight at Bradley. Rhodes followed suit, flicking his fuming glance to his number two. Both had heard the story.

*She was seventeen.*

*She had the tightest body, newly developed. If it weren't for the job, I would have ruined her for life. I would have fucked her in every hole, enjoyed every scream and moan. Instead, I had to cut the bitch and leave her bleeding, leave her for dead. I used a pair of scissors and sliced her face, gave her a proper Chelsea smile. When I stabbed her, it tore her cheeks something rotten. I bet she bled out on her little brother's carpet thinking of me.*

Bradley's face turned white in an instant. The sound of the voice punched him in the gut, crushing the air out of his lungs. He stumbled, placing a shaking hand on the wall to steady himself. Rhodes shook his head and loosened his tie, realising the problem that was arising here. "Dennis? Remind me."

"Dennis. Worked for you, wasn't very good at it. Had a wife and kids, two of whom you brutally murdered in a home invasion…sorry, hired someone to brutally murder. Ring a bell?"

Rhodes chuckled.

"Ah, yes. Dennis. Incompetent cunt that one. He got what he deserved, no one who works for me is a fucking liability," he spat, glaring at Bradley.

"Ah, but I disagree. How do I know this? Let's just say an eighteen-year-old girl outwitted two of your *best* men. Easily. You won't be seeing them again."

"Listen, *bitch*, I don't know who you think you are –"

"– right now, I'm your worst fucking nightmare. You sent someone to kill me and he didn't get the job done. You killed my family in cold blood. There will be severe consequences for that."

"This is hilarious," Rhodes quipped. "*Darling*, you have no idea who you're going up against, the magnitude of man power and security I have. Bring it, but you won't even get past the front gate."

"You don't have a front gate," the voice responded, almost instantly. "You have a compound, yes, but access is by helicopter or tunnel or on foot, if these schematics are anything to go by. I guess asking your lackeys to wipe their phones, or keep private documents elsewhere, wasn't in the brochure?"

Rhodes fell silent, a shadowy wave of crimson darkening his cheeks.

"And I have the access codes, a security card and everything I need to get in."

"You listen here –"

"– no, *you* listen, Rhodes. You put out a hit on my father. I saw my family die on your orders, on your command. Bradley didn't kill me, he let me survive on a whim charged by male bravado and bullshit, and because of this, I aim to bring you down. You can count on that."

Rhodes clenched his fist and punched the desk. The desk bounced, remaining unharmed. Blood oozed from a ruptured knuckle.

"You just signed your own death warrant, cunt."

"Maybe, but I have fuck all to lose, and that's because of you, no one else. Tell Bradley I said hello, and I will see him soon. As promised. He'll know what it means."

The caller hung up.

"Bradley, what the fuck…*arghhh*!" Rhodes slid his arms across his desk, sending its contents to the floor, several objects smashed against the wall with a loud crash. Rhodes stormed over to Bradley and pinned him against the wall, a knife to his cheek. "*What the fuck did you do?*"

Bradley swallowed, a bead of perspiration trickled down his face, his eyes on his boss, not the blade. "I gave her the Chelsea smile as...she challenged me so I fucked her up. I cut her cheeks with a pair of scissors and stabbed her in the gut. I pounded on her, almost broke her bones. She shouldn't have survived; she lost a shit load of blood."

"Newsflash, Sher-fucking-lock, she survived. You should have killed her, no loose ends. You know this; you know this better than *anyone*."

"I'm sorry, sir. I fucked up," Bradley stated.

Rhodes released his number two and pocketed his blade. He walked over to his desk. "Both of you bunk up; we have a fucking early start in the morning."

"You think Corey and Alan are still alive? You think she's bluffing?"

"No, she was telling the truth. There was something in that voice..."

"I'm surprised she can talk at all," Bradley chuckled. It didn't go down well, his laugh met with utter scorn from his companions. Rhodes hissed and tapped his landline handset. A dial tone filled the office. He dialled eleven digital chirps and waited, glancing around the office. The phone began ringing.

"I bet he's asleep," Bradley said dejectedly.

Andrews shook his head. "Who, Sanchez? I heard he doesn't sleep, like a proper sniper."

"Shut the fuck up, the pair of you, you're both on my fucking shitlist."

On the third ring, the phone was answered. "Yes?"

"Sanchez? I have a job for you."

"Certainly."

"It's urgent. I need you to do a trace on Cahill's phone."

"You know the fee," Sanchez said calmly, his Spanish accent mild, his English well spoken.

"Normal procedure, it'll be wired in an hour."

"Okay. Just the trace? I don't do babysitting like that fuck, Andrews. I'm not a taxi service or chauffeur either."

Andrews lunged in and stopped himself, covering his mouth. Rhodes nodded, smiling. "No, I need you go to the location and execute whoever is there."

"Even Cahill?"

"Yes, anyone. Use extreme prejudice. I need no survivors and no bodies. Get a cleaning crew, use a nuke, I don't care. Nothing can be traced back to me, understand?"

"Understood," Sanchez said. He hung up.

Rhodes looked at his men. "This bitch thinks she can fuck with us? She has another think coming. Bunk up."

# SIXTEEN

Dani's third shower in twelve hours did nothing to ease the burning guilt that currently consumed her. Despite the warm caress of the soapy water, and the sinus clearing steam, her muscles refused to relax, their tension bearing strain on her physical activity. She winced whenever she reached for something, groaned whenever she stood up too quickly.

She dried her hair with the same damp towel used after her previous showers, sighed and tossed it into the hamper. Her slick hair tickled her neck, rolling drops of water down her shoulders and back. She slipped a blue t-shirt over her wiry frame, one that stuck to the damp spots, rendering the ordeal more irritating than normal.

Dani closed her eyes, clamped her hands on the desk before her and breathed slowly.

*Calm down. You're just panicked and scared.*

*No, I'm guilty.*

*You have nothing to feel guilty about.*

*I killed two men in cold blood.*

*You killed the first two men of a murderous crew, a crew who partake in prostitution, drugs and firearms. They've murdered people, possibly hundreds – including your brother and mother, not to mention your father.*

*If you don't do something about it – especially now you've announced your existence to them – they will find you and they will kill you, not to mention hundreds of other people, anyone who gets in their way.*

*You're doing a little good in a world brimming with evil.*

*You knew the odds when you signed up for this.*

Dani sighed, her internal conflict coiling deep and complex in her stomach. She didn't relish what would come next, what bloody destruction was going to happen at her hands, but Dani knew she had no choice. It was kill or be killed.

She pulled her jeans up her legs and fastened them. Stepping to the bed, she ran her fingers along the Beretta, the one that had killed Alan with brutal efficiency.

*Brutal efficiency. You have nothing else.*

She had a plan, a blind plan, one that could change a hundred times by purely walking into the complex that belonged to Rhodes and his army. She knew it wouldn't be like any kind of fiction, nothing like a Schwarzenegger movie or those action films that take billions at the box-office. This would be sordid, uncomfortable, violent and sadistic. Blood would run in rivers and bodies would fall like raindrops.

*The sooner you become comfortable with that, the better.*

Dani shook her head and punched the wall, her fist cracking the cheap, hollow plaster. The pain shooting up her arm dulled immediately as she retracted her fist and flexed the hand outwards, dust and white plaster falling silently to the carpet.

A knock on the door made Dani stiffen.

Two raps – knock knock. Quick, efficient.

Not the normal three, slow raps of the next-door neighbour, one who had all the time in the world to letch and perve over Dani on a rare appearance. Only twice had he caught her out with an unlocked door, and never again would he catch her fresh from the shower.

The knock wasn't his, not motivated by lust or hormones. No, this was different.

It wasn't the rapid knocking of her postman who, on his first visit, was paid handsomely to knock six times fast on future visits. No one knocked six times; it was unheard of, the perfect code for a wary Dani. Besides, she hadn't ordered anything and no one knew where she lived, she paid her bills up front, a year in advance, and at the post office. She had no online presence, no digital footprint, and no mobile phone.

No, this was alien, normal. Someone on a schedule. Someone who would probably knock again in a moment, then leave if no reply was forthcoming.

Then, it hit her.

Dani's eyes scanned the room, almost in half speed, and fell on the phone on the bedside cabinet. The mobile phone, one with a lit up screen.

One that was active, a modern day homing beacon.

Alan's phone.

*How could I have been so dumb?*

Dani leapt from the ground onto her bed and pushed herself off the mattress, launching into the corner of the room. Seconds later, her front door exploded in a hail of silenced bullets and splintered wood. The gunfire obliterated the bed and the wall beyond it, puffing feathers and sharp plaster chips into the air. Dani landed with a crumple in the corner, her back objecting to the sudden impact, one that just saved her life. The stench of sulphur tickled her nostrils as she groaned, her body still aching.

The door swung inwards, loose on its broken hinges. A man walked through the entrance, a vicious MP7 submachine gun leading the way. He stepped into the apartment, his gaze fixed in front of him.

Grey smoke rose from the silencer and Dani wondered if anyone had heard the dangerous commotion.

She hoped not.

Dani pushed herself to a standing position and slid along the wall, still obscured by the door peppered with jagged holes, her fingertips gliding along the rough paint.

Through the largest hole – where the intruder had begun firing – she saw the man was Hispanic, with trimmed black hair, a coffee complexion and long brown coat. He stood about six foot tall and could have been anyone off the street. Dani noticed a unique blandness, a non-descript ordinariness to his appearance. In a crowd, nothing about him would stand out; nothing would alert someone to his presence.

He stepped beyond the door.

Dani pushed the door aside and the wood toppled off the damaged frame, hitting the carpet with a loud thud, alerting him. She ran forward, swung her left leg out and kicked the gun from the turning man's grasp. The weapon clattered against her bedside cabinet as she drove an elbow towards the intruder's face. He ducked, avoiding the blow, and swiped her one leg from under her, hoisting Dani into the air and launching her across the bed. Dani bounced off the mattress and rolled onto her feet, but her left foot slipped on the worn carpet. The man kneeled on the bed and drove a fist into her face, blasting stars across her blurred vision, knocking her to the ground.

The man laughed and stepped around the bed slowly. The door wobbled behind him, no longer in its frame, the last of the wood clattering to the carpet. Dani backed off, cornering herself. She pushed her back up against the wall behind her, poising her right foot against the flat surface.

The man chuckled again.

"I heard you were a fighter. I have to say, I'm pleasantly surprised."

Dani rubbed her nose gently, testing the throbbing flesh and bone. Nothing was broken. She fingered her scars on instinct and felt no pain there. The aches in her body subsided as adrenaline flooded into her bloodstream. "You must be Sanchez," she uttered.

"You did your homework, beautiful. Intelligence and brawn? Wow. If more women were like you, well, the world would be a vastly different place. No wonder Rhodes has a stick up his arse about you."

Dani said nothing.

"A quiet one I see? Have to admit, Bradley said otherwise about you, how you goaded him into letting you live. What a moron. Unlike him, you won't have that luxury with me." Sanchez reached behind him and closed his hand around a pistol in his belt.

Which is when Dani leapt.

Propelling herself from the wall, she swung a sharp elbow across her front, spinning her through the air. The most prominent bone on her body arced and lashed Sanchez across the face, shattering his nose and blinding him momentarily. He dropped the gun to the floor, clasping his hands to his broken face.

Dani hit the carpet and rolled, ending up behind her foe. She took the silenced pistol from the floor and poked it into the back of Sanchez's knee.

She fired.

Bone and sinewy cartilage sprayed across the room, pattering the wall. Huge globs stuck to the paint, some rolled down slowly. Sanchez screamed and collapsed backwards to the floor, his bloody hands coming away from his face. Dani leapt up and pinned her foe to the carpet.

Sanchez scrabbled for her face, so she broke his fingers, snapping each into a sickening right angle with a crack. Again, the man screamed, convulsing between her legs. Dani drove a sharp elbow down straight into his eye, shattering the eye socket and popping the eyeball with a soggy squelch, the yellow vitreous fluid shooting up into the air. Using both fists, she rained blow after blow into Sanchez's mutilated visage, splattering herself and the surrounding carpet with dark blood and vomit, which slowly seeped from the injured man's mouth.

Dani took a second to breathe. Sanchez murmured to himself, acidic bile and crimson bubbling from his damaged face. His left eye was swollen shut, his right eye a bloody, pus-filled gouge in a face rife with cuts and welts and puffy flesh. His hands slapped the carpet, his body reacting to the oncoming shock and escaping adrenaline.

Dani scooped up the gun again and pointed it at Sanchez's face. She blinked.

She fired, the bullet puncturing his forehead.

Sanchez ceased to move, his arms returning to the carpet and remaining there. Dani closed her eyes and breathed slowly. She than clasped her hands around the man's neck. Her bloody fingers slipped and careened on the slippery flesh as she struggled to find purchase. Eventually she did and gripped, squeezing the neck and jugular, closing off any possible oxygen to the dead man's brain. Her arms bulged with muscle, every inch of her body flexing its weight into her lethal grip, ensuring the man wouldn't come back. Dani felt her teeth aching as they pushed against one another, felt her neck muscles contract as she squeezed the corpse below her.

After five minutes, she released her grip and flopped back onto the carpet, sweaty and groggy. She wiped her face with a tingling forearm and stared at the intruder. Sanchez lay in a pool of dark blood and vomit. A foul stench polluted the air and Dani realised the body had voided its bowels.

Disgusted, she stood up and stumbled to the bathroom.

She lifted the toilet lid and vomited into the bowl. Once done, she leaned her sweaty forehead on her arm and groaned. After a moment, she felt a burning inside her, one she mistook for heartburn. It grew and bulged inside her, laboured her breathing, made her gag slightly.

There was no mistaking it.

The feeling was unadulterated rage.

Pure and simple.

The game had changed. Mere moments before, she'd felt guilty and hesitant, afraid to become one of them, what she assumed would be a regular feeling for anyone in her situation.

That was before; she was in the wrong place at the wrong time, an innocent bystander caught up in a murder, one she miraculously survived.

This time, it was different.

This time, it was pre-empted murder, an assassination attempt, a violation of her personal space – again – and a defiant show of retaliation from a man who was running scared from Dani, the one person who could bring his empire to the ground.

It changed the game.

This time, it was different.

And Dani now felt a difference, apathetic to her emotions and a moral compass. This man, the man responsible for bringing her life crashing to the ground, had to pay. No longer would she feel guilty for taking their lives, no longer would she doubt the violent actions of her vigilante justice.

No longer would she hesitate.

No longer would she fear Rhodes and his army. After all, she had nothing to lose because of him; he'd taken everything from her.

At that moment, her path became clear, a stark clarity laid her destiny before her.

*Would she die? Maybe. Would she suffer? Most likely.*

*Would she reap justice for her family? Totally.*

*Would she get revenge on those who wronged her? Yes.*

Dani smiled, the muscles of her face contorting her grin into a macabre grimace, one born of desperation and anger, one etched with payback. The young girl felt her sanity slip, her grip on reality fall to the wayside, and she welcomed it, felt a freedom that she'd never experienced before. Everything suddenly seemed brighter, more colourful, a lot less terrifying.

Teddy appeared in her mind's eye, his chubby face crying, then exploding and rewinding, she saw his young brain and skull spray outwards like a firework, like a small stick of dynamite had gone off inside his cranium, then climb back into her brother's reforming skull, like an exploding watermelon but in reverse. Dani saw the image repeat itself over and over and over.

Several times.

Dani gripped her temples, scratched and clawed at her skin, drawing blood, pulling hair from the roots.

She screamed; her face aimed at the ceiling, her neck muscles coursing with hot, boiling blood. Her eyes widened and she felt a chuckle escape her lips, a small laugh signaling her loss of grip on reality. She closed her eyes, exhausted.

She saw her mother's frail body obliterated by buckshot meant for an animal, saw her father die at Bradley's hand; his face caved in slowly and brutally by the man's huge weight and realised she hadn't actually seen this, but the image was so vivid and detailed and authentic, it seemed real. It knocked the wind from her rasping lungs, made her gasp and clutch her blood-soaked chest. Dani twitched and shuddered, but couldn't shake the images from her fragile mind, couldn't escape their macabre grasp and couldn't push the horrific, gruesome thoughts away. She saw the grotesque murder for what it was – a massacre.

Something clicked in Dani.

Something evil, something sinister, she felt the darkness coiling around her heart.

She opened her eyes and her consciousness was lost, shoved deep down in a shadowy shell of a woman with nothing left, who had nothing to lose.

A woman with one mission in life, one goal.

Revenge.

At any cost.

Laughing, Dani walked out of the bathroom. She picked up a black bag from the closet and exited the flat, leaving a trail of blood and death and destruction.

*It's time to end this.*

*It's time.*

# PART THREE

## Vengeance

# SEVENTEEN

"We haven't heard from Sanchez?"

Bradley ran a coarse hand through his hair and sighed, his weary eyes observing the picturesque scene before him. From his position on the balcony, he could see across the vast, foggy London landscape. The buildings stretched to the sky like dying fingers grasping at a lease for life. Off to the left, the unmistakable shape of the London Eye sat silently in the early mist, its circular shape beautiful and somewhat eerie in the morning haze.

Andrews sipped a coffee beside him, his overgrown lips slurping on the rim of the cup, the noise shattering the chilled elegance of the silent morning. Bradley shook his head; London only fell silent for a short time in the morning, normally between five and six, before the commuters and workers came out in sentient droves. Relishing the silence was one of life's little luxuries, one that was now lost on this morning. He shot a distasteful glance in his colleague's direction. "Sanchez will call. The woman doesn't stand a chance against him."

"You mean Dani?"

"Yes…Dani." Bradley narrowed his eyes and breathed in, the cool air caressing his lungs.

Andrews chuckled.

"It's okay, you can say her name. Just because you didn't kill her, just because you failed in your mission..."

"Fuck you," he spat.

"No, fuck *you*," Andrews retorted. "I'm not the stupid cunt who left a witness alive as part of a sick and demented game. I'm not the man who couldn't finish off a teenage *girl*. Fuck me; you're no better than Dennis."

Bradley said nothing.

He deserved the abuse.

Rhodes had hired him for a purpose and had given him the task because of his ruthless efficiency, a trait that appeared vacant during that part of the mission, one that now put their entire company in jeopardy. Bradley looked down on the empty streets of London and half expected to see Dani, the girl with the scars and stupid determination, looking back at him.

He wondered how long it would take her to arrive.

He knew she would.

He remembered that spark, that electricity in those young, immature eyes, one that spoke of persistence and a can-do attitude. He remembered her goading, remembered his own hormonal throbbing at how it turned him on, how he resisted the urge to do anything about it, how he refused to choke the kid out mid-fuck, and watch her eyes bulging in her bloody face as he filled her tightness with his seed.

He loved the feel of slick blood on his cock.

He closed his eyes, quickly pushing the image from his mind.

He steadied himself on the railing and breathed slowly. "She's mine."

Andrews sipped his coffee again, swallowing deeply. "Huh?"

Bradley cocked the Beretta in his hand and slid it into his holster. He breathed another lungful of frosty air and walked back into the tower. "When she gets here, I'm taking her down. This is my mess; I'm going to clean it up."

Andrews chuckled. "That's if Sanchez doesn't do the work for you."

\*\*\*\*\*

Dani stared at the metal floor of the tube carriage, her eyes tracing the lines of the design, focusing her for the task ahead. She noticed smeared mud and droplets of water, an indication of the early morning weather, evidence of the daily commute, the beginning of a typical London morning. The carriage clacked as they shot through another of London's many dark tunnels, the metal canister rocking sideways, jostling Dani in her seat.

She tugged at the pull cords that hung from the hood on her jacket, tightening them, hiding her face beneath the black material.

From her experience, tube passengers kept themselves to themselves, burying their one-track minds in books and phones and newspapers. No one made eye contact anymore, and no one started conversation.

The girl looked up and spotted two men, seats apart from each other, both silent. They wore cheap suits and both rustled a crinkled copy of *Metro* in their hands.

Rookies, up and comers.

The richer types usually wore long, luxury coats over their expensive suits, protecting their investment of a wardrobe from the harsh elements, a folded, pink *Financial Times* tucked beneath their moneymaking arm. They usually carried a leather briefcase and merged into the crowd as one, slipping between people with no effort and years of experience.

You could spot them a mile away.

These guys? They would push and shove people away, fight against the swelling of the London foot traffic. They didn't have a briefcase because they spent their starting salary on their commute and/or a local abode, if they didn't already fund an unwanted family or excessive lifestyle born from such a vocation.

Maybe some of them funded each of those things, but they were easy to spot, the routine of such a commute something they were yet to learn.

As if to confirm her point, the closest man knocked his lunchbox to the floor as he reached for his battered umbrella. The chaos that resulted from such an action saw him drop his newspaper, the umbrella clanged and rolled as it toppled to the floor and the man stumbled as he reached for the falling object all too late.

It concluded with him on his knees, checking the damage to this lunch, his hair unkempt from the cool air whistling through the open window in the doors beside him.

Dani pulled her eyes away and gazed out of the window, the dark tunnels whirred by, occasionally interrupted by an empty station that was surplus to their route, a prelude to her destination. She glanced at the map above the window, one crudely marked with a red outline of a bulbous penis, and realised she was three stops away.

*Three more stops.*

She estimated fifteen more minutes.

Her eyes dropped to the black bag between her legs, her mind counting the minutes off subconsciously, in time to the clacking of the carriage.

*Almost time.*

\*\*\*\*\*

"I'm not scared of a fucking teenager," Rhodes asserted, dropping an ice cube into a tumbler. He reached for a bottle of Jim Beam, unscrewed the lid, and poured two fingers into the glass. He sloshed the amber liquid around, the ice clinking against the sides, and turned back to his men.

"The day I become scared of a fucking teenager is the day I give up this company and that ain't fucking happening!"

Bradley nodded, as did Andrews. Both stood on the other side of his desk, awaiting instruction.

"I think we should double up on security, just in case," Bradley uttered. "I have a bad feeling about this."

Rhodes laughed, one gargled with mucus from a residing cough. He hacked, spitting a wad of green phlegm into his trash can. "You're serious, aren't you? You think this broad can do some serious damage?"

"I do, sir. She took out Corey and Alan. I wasn't their biggest fan, not by a long shot, but she got the drop on them pretty easily. They were competent at their job, efficient, if slightly liable. It rings alarm bells."

"It's not hard to outwit two drunk fucktards," Rhodes spat. Andrews stepped forward but was silenced by his angry boss, who held an open hand up in mock apology. Andrews stepped back, his head lowered. Rhodes sipped at his drink, hissing as the burning liquid warmed his dry throat. "It's not hard at all, but I suppose you have a point. Have we heard from Sanchez yet?"

Both men shook their heads, neither speaking.

"Hmmmm." Rhodes sat in his chair. He placed the glass on the table and dialled a number from his phone. After several speakerphone rings, he hung up. He necked the remaining bourbon and sighed. "Right, man the gates. Make sure all entrances are secure and as for the front door, and the reception area downstairs, I want it sealed off. No one in, no one out. Got it?"

Bradley nodded and left the room, going to work.

"Andrews, I want you downstairs, at the front door, take two men with you. Get three of your best men and have them commandeer the lobby outside, and gets some teams between here and the lifts. Got it?"

Andrews nodded.

"I don't think we'll need it, but you never know."

*****

Dani watched the street below, observed as people went about their business, their activities rendered silent by the double paned glass before her. A horn sounded somewhere in the distance and several cars of foreign origin silently crept by.

The world going about its business.

Her eyes flicked to the black tower before her.

Rhodes Enterprises, a structure standing forty floors tall, protected and maintained by a security crew of thirty-six, stood bleak and outright on the immaculate concrete opposite. The shape of the monstrosity reminded her of a giant black lava lamp, the glass sparkling in the early morning sunlight. She almost expected the middle windows to light up and amuse passersby with blobs of wax in hot water. It didn't, it just stood impassively, important and domineering above the businesses around it, they themselves shrouded in its shadow.

A front, a fake, a dummy corporation that housed an orgy of prostitution, drugs, arms dealing and murder, all hidden behind documentation of a financial loans company. She imagined he had cops and auditors, accountants and all manners of menial workers in his pocket.

*What bullshit*, Dani thought.

She gently massaged the puffy facial scars with her fingers, stroking the tips along the corrupted, blemished flesh. In times of stress, she found the action soothed her, but also reminded her of her failures, of the obstacles she'd overcome in life. The tragedy that changed her scope on everything was crammed into the span of four-hundred or so days, but it felt a lot longer.

She remembered laying in the hospital bed, wondering if she would ever be the same, if she would ever cherish the experience of a prom or a faithful boyfriend, a relationship or a marriage and parenthood, or even some resemblance of normalcy ever again.

Dani held onto that hope for the entire duration of rehab, for an entire sixty-three days.

She refused to look in a mirror, outright declined a look at her mutilated reflection for that period, the very thought of which threatened to push her over the edge and send her swirling into a mass depression.

Therefore, she lived every day positively, the shred of lingering hope that her face would heal naturally, in line.

She remembered how crucial it was that her severed tissue and muscle lined up, how they utilised the sutures to coax the separated flesh back together, like two sheets of material. The memory returned of how important those first few days were in order to maintain her visage, to reduce the scarring and ensure her facial functions returned to normal.

The many nurses and doctors, all of whom blurred into one on the back of heavy medication and advanced surgical procedures, identity-covering masks and outfits, were her rock, the one thing keeping her going.

In the final days, she faced her fear head on, chancing a shot at redemption, facing her worst thoughts in a hope to get on with her life.

She dreamed of moving on, relocating, finding a job, possibly finishing school and making something of her life, to do her family proud.

Of course, at that point, she didn't realise just how the events had transpired, how her father was the reason for her life crumbling to the ground before it started.

When she set eyes on her scarred face, she knew her life would never be the same.

Not one iota of her life would return to normal.

Dani felt a surge, a rush of hot blood to the brain. Her life came crashing down around her at that very moment, in that lavender scented hospital bed. In that moment, walls crashed around her, school vanished into the distance, one specked with blood, dead rotting bodies and terrifying fear and loss.

She was no longer a normal teenager. Her dreams of a prom and a husband and a life, of an education and normalcy, were long gone, burnt to a crisp at the very sight of her mutilated, horrendous reflection.

Dani didn't cry.

Dani didn't feel anything.

Up to that point, the only mystery that scared her was the unveiling of a report card or a duff Christmas present from an out-of-touch relative. The revelation of her visage was something wholly different, entirely horrendous.

It was the moment she realised her life was over.

Only after her discharge, weeks later, did she realise that DI Scott was such an important presence, a faded image on the cusp of her drug-induced state. After a conversation with a doctor, she discovered that the officer had stopped by three times a week, sometimes more, to see her during rehabilitation, to ensure she made it back to health. She remembered a genuine warmth emanating from the gesture, one lacking since no family members had come to see her, to check on her welfare. As for Scott, she always made it her mission to see him again, to thank him for his support, as anonymous and unrealised as it was.

She never did.

She closed her eyes and placed his crumpled business card on the table beside her.

She might still get that chance.

But first, she had work to do.

Dani opened her eyes and turned to the items on the hotel bed behind her. She gazed over the equipment positioned across the flowery duvet and closed her eyes again, memorising the arsenal at her disposal.

A bulletproof vest, complete with underclothing, skintight. Two MK7 submachine guns, silenced and double-clipped. Two hundred rounds each. Two silenced Berettas with three clips each, containing 9mm parabellum bullets.

A SPAS 12 shotgun with extendable stock and fifty shells.

Three hand grenades.

A bowie knife.

Dani looked at the black bag, one that would allow easy access to all of the weapons, and smiled. She felt the tug of her scars.

The woman turned back to the window and gazed across the street.

*They did this to you.*

*To Mom.*

*To Teddy.*

*To Dad.*

*They took your life away from you; they ruined your future and massacred your family. They destroyed you.* Dani felt a salty tear rolling down her cheek and didn't swat it away. She let it flow and swallowed when she realised something.

Dani was no more.

Dani used to be an innocent young girl with a bright future and a doting family.

That girl died in her brother's bedroom that night, she just held on too long, a passenger who missed their stop.

*You've been fighting and fighting. Now, the moment has arrived.*

Now, she was no one, an anonymous blotch on the landscape of life.

She was vengeance.

She was payback.

Dani smiled, a darkness tempering her eyes, consuming her.

*You're no longer Dani – you're something else.*

*You have a new name, one that will begin its reign of terror today.*

As the last shreds of sanity slivered away, leaving the hotel room and Dani's consciousness for the final time, the woman cackled to herself.

*You are something...*

"Grin," she uttered. "I am Grin."

# EIGHTEEN

Detective Chief Inspector Scott dropped the greasy bag of breakfast on his desk and walked to the window. He breathed out slowly, his coffee-tinted breath steaming the glass before him. He smiled and wiped the pane with his sleeve.

*Another day in paradise.*

His view wasn't spectacular; it gazed straight onto the back of a red brick building, such was the lack of space in a modern metropolis like London. Occasionally, he would see the cleaners vacuuming the carpets or bear witness to a meaningless, silent meeting between entitled speakers and bored, cash-strapped employees. Yes, the theatre that was car insurance really provided a break away from the debauchery and darkness of crime.

*Could be worse*, he thought. *I could sell car insurance for a living.*

*Much worse if you were one of the managers who feel their spiel and corporate agenda actually matters for shit. Everyone can see a manager for their true form – a corporate patsy with brains that are more washable than a teenager's crusty bedsheets.*

Scott chuckled and turned away, returning to his chair. "I'll settle for *this* type of criminal, thank you very much."

He tore the brown bag down the side, not wanting to smear the grease on his fingers. The smell of crispy bacon and grilled sausage tantalised his senses. He pressed the button on his laptop and watched it power up. As the technology hummed awake, he lifted his breakfast bap from the bag and took a large bite. Brown sauce enveloped his tongue, igniting the flavour in the crunchy bacon and tender sausage meat.

"Amazing, as always."

Scott tapped a key on his laptop and watched the blank, blue screen illuminate. It prompted him for a password. Before he could enter it, a rap on his door alerted him.

"Yeah, come in."

A rotund woman with greasy brunette hair and a waddle in her step – the downfall of a sedentary lifestyle – entered the room. She adjusted her brown skirt and stood, arms crossed, a little cautious. "Sir, sorry to bother you –"

"– it's quite alright, Megan, I just got in. Can I help?"

"Just got in? I can come back?"

"No, its fine. I'm catching up on my breakfast," he chuckled. "How can I help?"

"Well, this is weird…but we got a call for you."

"That's fine, send it to my phone," he uttered, lifting his receiver in preparation.

Megan pushed her glasses up her nose.

"No, the person is gone. They left a message, about ten minutes ago."

Scott turned to the woman, his attention averted. "A message?"

"Yes."

"I can call them back, got a number?"

"That's just it, sir."

Megan took a step forward, as it to emphasise the point. "The call didn't come through to your phone and they didn't leave a number."

"That's not unusual, not everyone has my direct line," Scott said, replacing the receiver.

"Well...this...um...it came through on your old number. Your DI number."

Scott frowned. "Okay, I thought it was linked to my new number."

"It is, but the call came through Duggan's desk. I think you'd better listen to it, sir."

"Sure thing. Is it on the database?"

"Yep, I lined it up for you."

"Did Duggan listen to it?"

"No, Duggan is on leave."

"Probably in rehab..." Scott sighed, his head lowering, remembering his own alcoholic demons. He pushed the memory away.

"Everything okay, sir?"

"Yeah, I'm fine. Thanks for letting me know, Megan."

"No problem," the woman responded, smiling. She turned and left the office. Scott took a huge sip of coffee, entered his password and clicked a folder icon on his desktop.

Several calls, in the form of files with a $C$ on them, appeared on the screen. Scott found the one he needed and double clicked it. The file opened into a black box with a timer at the bottom and a blue quaver note on the screen. Scott fumbled with his headphones and put them in his ears.

After a muted hissing, the call began.

After a moment, Scott's eyes widened and he felt the heat flush from his face. A mild panic startled to bubble in his stomach as he scrambled for his car keys, knocking his coffee to the floor. The cup spiraled and spattered the carpet with frothy brown spots. As the call ended, he dropped his headphones to the desk with a clink.

"Shit."

He stood up, rubbing his face, his thought process in overdrive.

As he ran out of the office, his mobile phone tucked beneath his chin, he beckoned to several officers to follow him. Thirty seconds later, he was requesting more back up from his vehicle, the words from the call reverberating through his skull.

\*\*\*\*\*

*This is a message for Detective Inspector Scott. You may remember me – my name is Dani.*

Dani stepped out of the hotel lobby and onto the wet pavement. The rain had let up slightly, but the chilled dampness of the air still irritated her scarred skin. Brushing her cheek, she pulled the hoodie across her face and looked both ways at the hurried pedestrians, most of whom were making their way to work.

After a moment she walked forward, her boots clonking on the hollow concrete, and stepped into the road, ignoring the BMW that screeched to a halt on her left.

The driver's frantic screaming went unheard, her brain totally in the zone.

*You questioned me over the death of my family over a year ago.*

She patted the top of a black bollard as she walked towards Rhodes Enterprises, the weight of her dual Berettas a comfort as they tapped her spine, her tight jeans pushing them into the small of her back. The hoodie that concealed them started to dampen, the returning rain thudding on her shoulders. Her feet paused as she reached the steps, realising that, once she started her ascent, there was no going back.

"This is it, the plan coming to fruition," she whispered to herself.

She tightened the hood around her face and started forward.

*I never thanked you for remaining vigilant by my side during my rehabilitation. I blame the drugs, but there is no excuse for forgetting your kindness, something that wasn't your responsibility at all, but that was still provided to me in my time of need.*

Leaving the steps behind, Dani pushed the revolving door and slowly entered the monolith of a tower block.

The door span silently as the sounds of the street – footsteps, vehicles chugging by, a distant police siren – vanished, the walls merging behind her.

*Your kindness was a beacon of hope, one that has led me to this very moment, spurred me into action, and enabled me to take revenge against those that took everything from me.*

The lobby carried a fragrant smell of coffee. Dani scanned the minimalist room, searching for a Costa or Starbucks, or one of the chain stores that normally leeched off addicted employees with a convenient fixture in the foyer. Four leather sofas, two on each side, flanked the entrance, accompanied by glass coffee tables with time-passing magazines on their flawless surfaces. Before her stood two escalators, one going up and one coming down, both secured behind a metal detector fixed between two sturdy wooden counters. She took a step forward and, in that moment, the picture before her changed.

*Anyway, you said the lead ran cold on the perpetrators...I can reveal that if you go to Rhodes Enterprises in Tottenham Court Road, you will find your answers.*

Three men stood up behind the right counter, their coats bulging with the unmistakable indentation of a weapon. Three sets of eyes watched the new arrival intently. After a moment, two men stepped around the desk and made their way towards Dani slowly, who placed her hands on her hips, her eyes staring at the marble tiles beneath her feet.

"Sorry, miss, Rhodes Enterprises is closed for maintenance today." The man on the left bit into a green apple, the crunch echoed around the lobby.

Dani nodded, still looking down. "I have a meeting with Ross Rhodes."

The man on the right chuckled. "He's unavailable today. May we reschedule your meeting?"

Dani glanced up, her smile stretching her scars into an absurd grimace, a grin bearing horrific memories and sadistic violence.

"Gross," the man said grimacing, his mouth still chewing the fruit.

"Fuck, what happened to your –"

"– *it's her!*" The man behind the counter screamed, his finger aimed in their direction. The sudden shout caused both of his comrades to turn away from Dani.

*Perfect*, she thought, her hands sliding behind her.

*FYI, I'm already headed there so I apologise for any mess I cause.*

Dani drew both silenced Berettas and kneeled, placing one barrel beneath the chin of each distracted man. Without hesitation, she pulled the triggers.

*Yours, Dani.*

*Whup.*

The back of the left man's head exploded outward, the top of his skull splintering into the air, bone fragments and greyish pink brain matter spurted across the lobby like wet confetti. Chunks of soggy apple dribbled from between his lips; followed by blood and shattered teeth as the bullet discharged through solid muscle, brittle bone and soft tissue, ripping through his mouth, killing him instantly.

*Whup.*

The right man fared slightly differently. Still turning as the gun fired, the bullet shattered his larynx; muscle and cartilage obliterated beneath the bullet, a heavy red mist sprayed into the copper-infused air. His jaw, devastated by the close-quarters blast, flopped to one side, hanging from his mutilated face by ripped tendons and blood-soaked sinew. Crimson dripped and sluiced in heavy patters, filling the lobby with a cacophony of splashes.

Both men flopped to the floor heavily, landing beside one another. Dani pumped another bullet into the remainder of each man's dying brain, for good measure. She stood up, wiping a smear of blood from her cheek, which only daubed it across her already menacing visage.

The woman walked swiftly towards the counter with both guns by her side.

The third man, gagging from the stench of sulphur and coppery blood, tumbled to the floor, the counter no longer protecting him.

He pointed his weapon at Dani haphazardly, the aim all over the place. Dani smiled. "Nice to meet you, Philip Andrews."

Andrews stared up, leaning on his elbows, surprised that she knew his name. He fumbled his gun, the handle slipping from his trembling hand.

"My father noted that you were nothing but a glorified babysitter. Seems he was right."

Andrews sneered. "Fuck you."

Dani chuckled. "Never been in a gunfight, huh? Too bad. That's the problem with being a babysitter, or nothing but a lackey, giving orders for orders sake." She leaned forward, snatching the gun from him. She looked it over and grinned. "You forgot to take the fucking safety off."

Clicking the safety, Dani fired three times, each bullet smacking Andrews in the chest with a muted thud, a spray of dark blood spat from each wound. The man's body rocked, as if fried by an electrical current, and he dropped to the floor. Dani shot him in the head, finishing the job. She tossed his weapon to the ground. It skittered across the floor and thudded against the counter.

She glanced around, listening, awaiting the arrival of more men. It didn't happen. She ambled behind the counter, stepping over the dead body, and starting looking at the files there. Ears alert, she continued to listen. Only a subtle gurgling from the three corpses sounded in her ears. Nothing stood out as she rifled through the files, so she looked up.

The security monitors showed forty floors of long hallways and mostly empty boardrooms. Some rooms housed several men, all equipped with firearms, some alert, some distracted with their mobile phones or magazines. Towards the bottom of the screen sat a derelict basketball court adorned with several cabins.

Three half-naked women milled around, hugging one another, drinking coffee and smoking.

Dani tapped a button on the screen and the image disappeared, filtering in six more small squares against a backdrop of black.

She saw an office, extravagant in its size.

A man sat behind a vast desk, drinking from a tumbler. Dani had never set eyes on Rhodes before but she *knew* it was the gangland boss - he exuded wealth and power. Another shot showed an entrance lobby, where three soldiers, two men and a woman, stood silently.

Waiting.

She felt a smile tugging at her scars.

She stood up and walked to the lifts.

*****

"Excuse me for asking, sir, but why the urgent rush?"

DCI Scott veered his Astra around a crawling Audi and rejoined the traffic on Weymouth Street. The magnetised blue siren on the roof howled, beckoning for a right of way, but some lapse drivers were determined to make his journey harder, such was the way in the capital.

DI Howes pushed back and braced herself against the passenger seat to avoid falling forward. "Are you trying to get us fucking killed?"

Scott said nothing as he spun the steering wheel and turned into Harley Street, in an attempt to avoid some of the traffic that was bringing Weymouth to a grinding halt.

The road was much clearer as he hurtled towards his destination. He noticed a few muted screams of people transfixed by the speeding vehicle and the blaring siren. The curious gaze of the general public saw him hurtle by.

"I have a lead on Ross Rhodes," Scott finally confessed.

A flicker of recognition appeared on the young DI's face, one that reduced the peppered red hue on her cheeks. She brushed a stray strand of hair from her face. "*The* Ross Rhodes?"

"Yep," Scott retorted, clenching the steering wheel.

"Nice one."

A smile of trepidation spread across Howes' face.

"You ready to become fucking famous, Howes?" Scott asked, smiling.

"Fuck no, sir. Who would be suicidal enough to tip the police about Rhodes...surely the person knows he has coppers in his pocket, right? Well, if the rumours are true."

"They're true, Howes, but I don't think this woman gives a shit, with all due respect. This girl lost everything because of Rhodes; she saw her family brutally slaughtered at the hands of his employee. I met her once, poor girl. Seventeen and she saw her brothers head...well, it wasn't pretty."

"How comes I never heard of her?"

"This was some time ago, before your transfer. A year ago, she vanished, just disappeared. Until this morning, I hadn't heard from her since our last interview. It was in the newspapers of course, back then, it must've made her a social outcast, but those things die down very quick nowadays. The first call I get from her, in a year, thanks me for being by her side and confesses to walking into the fucking lion's den. Talk about mixed emotion in a phone call. Rhodes left this girl humiliated and mutilated...it's not going to be pretty."

"You stood by her side?" Howes queried.

"Throughout the whole ordeal. She had no one, no interested family members. Rehab took about two months."

"That's mighty kind of you, sir."

"Just doing my duty, Howes. Questioning her afterwards was awkward; it felt like I was only supporting her to get information about her tragedy."

"She obviously didn't see it like that."

"I know," Scott uttered. "Now, she's walking into a certain deathtrap to avenge her family."

"I understand that, but surely she isn't psychopathic enough to just walk up to Rhodes and blow his head off?"

Scott looked across at his companion and said nothing.

Howes gulped, the silence speaking volumes, and looked out of the window at the passing scenery. The DCI turned onto New Cavendish Street, the screeching tyres the only sound that filled the cab.

# NINETEEN

Dani stood to the side of the lift, her shoulders brushing against the steel interior. As she moved closer to the metal entrance, to scope for potential noise, her coat brushed several numbered buttons, turning them orange.

As the car came to a gradual halt, gravity squeezing on her shoulders as the speed decreased, she breathed in and stood back, the Beretta in her left hand poised.

The doors slid open silently.

Nothing happened.

No bullets clattered into the lift. No one attacked.

Keeping her finger on the open button, she nudged sideways, peering into the quiet entrance hallway of the fortieth floor. No one stood watching, no armed gunman were awaiting her certain execution. She tapped the button once more and slid from cover, her feet padded by the lush black carpet. The doors closed shut behind her.

The hallway before Dani stretched forward, the rosy red walls etched with symmetrical doorways and tasteful, expensive art. Dani recognised magnificent pieces from Monet, Picasso, Klimt and Dalí. The end of the hallway finished with an expansive floor-to-ceiling window.

Dani could see the grey clouds and dull sky beyond, the rain pattering silently against the pane. Much like the foyer on the ground floor, dual leather sofas decorated each side of the reception area surrounding the lifts, a large square of space intended to feel welcoming and comfortable en route to an interview or a meeting or certain death.

Dani walked forward, listening intently, placing her bag of weapons on one of the sofas. Muted murmurs came from a room to the right. She tried to remember the layout from the blueprints and cursed herself for not checking them before leaving the hotel. She did remember the layout of the floor was like a staggered figure of eight, and the lifts were in the centre of it. The hallway looped around gradually behind the lifts. That's where Rhodes' office sat, protected by several walls built around it. No direct lift access meant anyone meeting him would have to run the gauntlet of his army.

Including her.

Dani breathed out and started forward.

The second lift dinged behind her, catching her off guard.

As she turned, she saw a man emerge in a hurry, his arms cradling several greasy brown bags. The stench of fast food permeated the air as he stepped onto the plush carpet. It took a second for his eyes to latch onto the intruder.

In seconds, he dropped the bags, and reached for a hidden weapon. Dani ran towards him quickly, darting left then right, confusing the man as she sprang, her foot catching the side of his knee, cracking the collateral ligaments, snapping the leg sideways. The man, his face bleaching white from immense agony at the explosion on his patella, howled seconds before Dani rammed her firearm into his face, silencing him.

His nose crunched beneath the weapon, spilling warm blood across his cheeks. The man collapsed backwards into the lift with a tremendous clang, his body crashing heavily into the car, bouncing it a few feet down. Dani landed on top of him, ready to silence him again.

It wasn't needed. The car regained its normal position.

She pulled a bowie knife and slid the blade into his neck, slicing through flesh and muscle, cutting the jugular. Blood began to spurt from the wound, so Dani pulled his collar up over his face. With the sound of gushing blood in her ears, she breathed a sigh of relief.

*One more down.*

Dani was on her feet in seconds and exited the lift just as three men entered the hallway.

Exclaims of surprise and shock filled the air. Two men lifted their weapons – Dani noticed they were M16 assault rifles, extremely lethal in close quarters – and dived behind one of the sofas. A single gunshot shattered the quaint elegance of the room and the leather arm exploded above Dani's head, puffing cotton and shredded chips of wood onto her hoodie. She swiped the hood down, requiring her entire peripheral vision, and ducked out of range. The smell of gunpowder tickled her nostrils.

The man held a hand up to his comrades. "You might as well come out, there's nowhere to go."

Dani listened, her options limited.

The bulk of her bulletproof vest rubbed against her creased waist, restricting her movements. She could feel sweat trickling down her sides, itching her neck. "I'm just here for Ross Rhodes. Leave now and I'll let you all live."

Howling laughter erupted from the men. The third man slapped his companion on the shoulder as the men whittled down. "Bitch, I don't think you *know* who Ross Rhodes is. Come out and we won't kill you," the leader said, winking at his fellow soldiers. Both raised their weapons. "Come out or we'll come to you."

She found herself laughing under her breath. "Last warning. I want Rhodes. No one else has to die," Dani said, checking her ammunition. Both pistols were at full capacity, something she had ensured in the lift ride up. Her pockets, now less heavy, jangled with loose bullets.

"Fuck you."

"Yeah, fuck you, whore, we ain't no docile husband you can boss around."

Dani nodded. "Have it your way."

She stood up, something that surprised the men, something that shocked her. The men all held M16's, all pointed in her direction. She was a dead woman walking.

The element of surprise gave her crucial seconds.

Dani shot the third man, the furthest away, in the face. His skull staved in on itself with a soggy crack, blood and brains and teeth splattering onto the wall beside him. He collapsed, dead before he hit the ground, his blood-spattered torso careening into a small table adorned with a pot plant, which toppled and hit the floor with a muted thud.

Dani double tapped the nearest man in the leg, bringing a howl of terror and agony from the soldier as he flopped awkwardly to the ground, dropping his weapon as his hands shot to the hole in his thigh. The second man, stunned by the reflexes of such a small woman, hesitated. Dani shot the fallen man in the head quickly then aimed at the second man, stopping him in his tracks.

"Don't," she said. She collected the fallen M16 from the floor and looped the strap over her shoulder.

He didn't. The man placed his weapon on the floor and held his hands outwards, signaling surrender. Dani smiled, the scars tugging once more.

She bent down and released the magazine from the second weapon, kicking it aside.

"Do you know who I am?"

The man shook his head, his eyes not leaving Dani's mutilated face.

She glanced down the hallway, expecting reinforcements at any second. She pocketed the magazine. "Did your boss not brief you?"

He shook his head again. Dani narrowed her eyes, prompting a vocal response. "N…no, he just said not to let anyone up here. To kill on sight."

"Well...you failed, that goes without saying. What will Rhodes do to anyone who...failed him?" Dani stepped in close, pushing her grinning face into the man's personal space, her wide eyes on him every inch of the way. She began circling him slowly, tapping him with her silenced Beretta gently on his leg, his back, then his arm and finally his chest. "Will he kill you?"

The man nodded.

"Will he...do this to you?" Dani jabbed at her face with the Beretta, the cooling silencer marking her bloodied cheek with gun residue. She ran it along her scars, the metal tingling the blemished skin somewhat. "Will he?"

The man shook his head again, sweat trickling down his face. "I don't...don't know."

"He did this to me. *This* is your boss' handiwork. Do you agree with his principles? Mutilating teenagers and slaughtering children in their homes, innocent children?"

"Lady, I –"

"– do you agree with his principles?" She asked, interrupting her foe.

He stared at the woman, his brain bouncing in his skull, panic making him tremble. The urge to vomit, brought on by the puffy scars across the woman's face, was immense. "No," he uttered finally, defeated.

"So, why do you work for him?"

The man shrugged, saying nothing. Dani pistol-whipped him, breaking his cheekbone with an audible crack. He stumbled to one knee, holding his face. "You crazy *bitch*!"

"Why do you work for *him*?"

"I don't know, *I don't know*. You're insane!"

"Trust me, this is me being civil. Tell me, soldier, do you possess a comms device, a way of communicating with the other men?"

Spitting blood and a tooth to the carpet, he nodded. "Yes," he said flatly.

Dani smiled. "And how many of you are there?" She pointed to the ground and waved her arm around. "Not counting these unfortunate gentlemen, obviously."

The man licked his lips. "Forty –"

"– if you lie to me, I will blow your bollocks off, got that?"

"Twenty one…nineteen not including Keith and Michael." His eyes wandered to his fallen comrades.

"And that gentleman?" Dani pointed to the lift, its door opening and closing against the protruding leg that stuck out awkwardly. Several hamburgers lay scattered on the carpet. She saw resignation in the man's face, his broken, swelling cheek fused with defeat. "Eighteen."

"What's your name?"

The man hesitated. "Furlong."

She watched the man, and realised he was telling the truth. "If you want to live, Furlong, I need you to do something."

"I'm dead anyway, doesn't seem I have much of a choice."

Dani said nothing.

\*\*\*\*\*

"Did you hear that?"

Doug Rinaldi wiped his trembling lips, smearing cold sweat across his palm. The nauseating tendrils of a hangover pulled and poked at his brain, making him feel hot and irritable. The slightest sound multiplied to the roar of a jet engine flying overhead. At first, he thought he was imagining things, and he covered his ears at the deafening blast, but the startled reaction of his comrades told him otherwise.

"Did you hear that? That wasn't me imagining things, was it?"

Lewis Gilson, his arms crossed, his yellow teeth gnashing a wad of gum, looked at his friend and nodded. "A single gunshot from an automatic weapon?

That's Michael's MO, he's very fussy about his ammunition. Sounds like our visitor is here."

Rinaldi adjusted his cap for the seventh time. "How do you know it's an automatic weapon?"

Gilson sneered. "Practice. I'd know that sound anywhere."

Rinaldi gulped. "Shouldn't we go help or something?"

Gilson shook his head. "We've been ordered to stay put, no matter what. We protect Mr Rhodes and we don't leave this room unless that phone rings. Andrews' orders."

Rinaldi eyed the black phone on the corner desk. Normally a busty blonde receptionist, handpicked by Rhodes, would be sitting there, her undone blouse – or the bulging contents of such a wardrobe choice – providing a welcome distraction to visitors. Rinaldi swallowed, his alcohol parched tongue making him cough. "What if they're dead?"

Gilson laughed. "Who, Team Four? Give me a break."

Kindra Sowder chuckled. "You moron. We're up against a teenage *girl*. What's the worst she could do, blind us with her selfie taking skills?" She buffed her M16 with a shirtsleeve, the lethal weapon laid across her thighs. "That woman is walking into a world of bloody hurt. She's outmanned and outgunned. I don't even know why we have so many people on this."

Rinaldi nodded frantically. "Didn't you start for Rhodes when you were nineteen?"

Sowder nodded. "Yes, but I'm fucking awesome. One of a kind."

Gilson laughed, his eyes pinned on the door. "One day, Sowder, you'll give me a rematch. Then you won't be so awesome. One day."

"Better get down the gym, pronto. Can't be losing an arm wrestling contest to a woman twice in a month. I doubt your misogynistic pride could handle that."

"Fuck you," he retorted, smiling.

"In your wildest dreams," she spat instantly. She slammed a magazine into the M16 and stood up, brushing her trouser legs.

"Do we really have to sit here? I want to kill shit."

"Easy there, Bundy," Gilson uttered. "You'll get your chance. Well, if she makes it this far."

Rinaldi sat in silence, listening, his head booming with every miniscule sound. "I think someone is coming."

Sowder eyed her colleague nervously. "I can't hear a thing. How much did you drink last night?"

"Too much. How was I to know Rhodes would call me in on my day off?"

"You knew the risks when you signed up. Still, beats being a copper, eh?"

"Until four weeks ago, I *was* a fucking copper," Gilson interjected. "I don't miss it, joining Rhodes was the best decision I ever made. The amount of coppers I knew who lived in fear of our boss...man, it made the job so hard. The wage was fuck all, not worth the risk."

"Explains a lot," Sowder joked. Gilson rolled the gum around his tongue, poking it out at his female counterpart. She said nothing.

Rapid gunfire made all three soldiers stand to attention.

The muted thuds of lethal projectiles hitting unseen objects became a dull soundtrack of broken noise within seconds. Squeals and shouts of pain and agony pierced the noise, providing brief intermissions.

The sounds of slaughter filled the small lobby.

"Remember, hold your ground," Gilson said, his gun aimed at the double wooden doors before him. He shot a wary glance at Sowder, who nodded. She slid behind an overturned desk with her weapon propped and aimed. Rinaldi crawled behind Gilson, hands pinned to the sides of his head.

Silence filled the room.

Then, the phone rang.

*****

Dani dropped the bullet-ridden body of Furlong to the blood-drenched carpet. She staggered to the wall and leaned against it gratefully, her breath coming in ragged gasps. Her blood-soaked palms gained no purchase on the surface, so she held them out before her, pushing with her back. She rubbed them on the damp carpet sharply, one that was quickly guzzling the blood from eight fresh corpses.

Her idea had worked, but it wasn't without severe consequences.

Her main concern was the noise.

And the hole in her arm.

Due to the fracas, there was no doubt that every remaining soldier – eleven by Furlong's previous count – would now be on high alert. Dani stepped over his punctured body and moved towards the corner, the branch of the hallway that would take her to Rhodes.

She sagged, leaning against the wall.

She wanted to close her eyes, take a breather, just for one second.

The idea has been simple. After Furlong explained the setup to her, under duress from a Beretta in his ear, she understood there were four teams. She'd dismantled Team Four on her exit from the lift. Team One was assigned with protecting Rhodes, so that left Two and Three. She'd forced Furlong to radio his fellow men, asking them to change tactics and supply reinforcements to his team, and they'd promptly arrived.

The order in which they arrived had nearly been her downfall.

Whilst standing in the middle of a long hallway, team two emerged from the front and team three from a rear doorway, boxing them into a narrow hallway. Dani couldn't help but notice the sly smile on Furlong's face, an indication that he had deceived her. Dani bit her lip and surveyed the odds – three men on one side, four on the other, all aiming a variety of weapons at the defenseless woman. Furlong leaned in close, goading. "You're screwed now, bitch. *Fuck you.*"

Dani realised she *was* screwed, a dead woman, until Furlong did something extremely stupid.

He turned his back on her.

So, Dani shot him in the back of the knee.

Furlong screamed as sinew and cartilage flapped into the air, spattering the wall. He tumbled backwards, on top of Dani as she slipped to the ground. The man span, not wanting to land on his back, and pinned Dani to the floor, unintentionally protecting her from gunfire.

She elbowed him in the face, dazing him, and fired, hitting one of the men to the rear.

The bullet powered into his shoulder, crushing the clavicle, the muscle and bone destroyed by the projectile, ripping as the lead tore through with no effort. He whipped around, his loose trigger finger spraying bullets at his team, killing them both. One of the other men fired his shotgun, a chain reaction from the close assault, blowing the first man's head off in a splurge of red mist, his head disintegrating behind the buckshot. Dani watched as the two other men were punctured and rag dolled by the close proximity of the automatic weapon, the friendly, accidental fire quickly destroying them and turning them into ragged piles of bloody mush. All three men flopped to the floor, dead and mutilated. Bullets embedded in the wall were still smoking.

She knew she'd got extremely lucky, but she didn't have time to pause and rest on her laurels. The teams wouldn't risk killing Furlong, or each other, in a crossfire, but that was no longer the situation.

Dani span on her stomach, hoisting Furlong off her back, positioning him in front of her as a shield. One man fired, taking a risk, the bullet glancing her exposed arm, tearing the skintight suit and hoodie with ease.

The flesh erupted; blood sluiced from the narrow valley that shredded the skin and muscle. Wincing, she fired again, her aim seriously compromised by the wound. The bullet glanced off the wall harmlessly.

The four remaining men all took up offensive positions. Furlong groaned before her, his arms beginning to find their function again. Using the butt of her Beretta, she rapped him viciously on the back of the head and swapped hands. Furlong sagged with a grunt.

"If you don't give up, we'll kill you."

"All you guys do is fucking talk," she said, and fired at them. Again, the bullet fired wide, shattering a picture on the wall. The frame crunched to the carpet. The nearest soldier stepped around it.

Dani wiped hot droplets of sweat from her brow and realised her hair was damp, her neck slick with warm perspiration. Her vision began to blur at the edges, so she slapped herself, realising the peril of the situation. Her arm was on fire, the pain becoming unbearable. Her fingertips began to numb so she shook her arm. It felt like waving a heavy log in a strong wind.

"Give up. Now."

"I'm here for Ross Rhodes —"

Furlong began to shake in front of her, struggling, his arms flapping, his elbows driving into her sides. She attempted to cover her head before one blow knocked her injured arm. Dani hissed, the pain searing through her body, white-hot agony paralyzing her for mere seconds. Furlong struggled to his feet, kicking Dani away.

She was exposed. Furlong ran to his comrades. "Shoot the bitch, *do it*."

Dani knelt on the carpet, fully at their mercy. Her left arm hung limp, blood soaking her torn sleeve. Her right hand gripped her Beretta, the second abandoned on the carpet behind her.

Furlong continued to stumble forward and leaned against the wall. "What are you waiting for?"

One soldier nodded, his head bobbing a mess of red hair, and ambled forward. He pulled a pistol from his holster and aimed at Dani. "You had it coming."

She smiled, the muscles tugging on her scars.

He fired.

The bullet smashed into Dani's chest, sending her sprawling.

"Ha!" Furlong said, bouncing, pointing at the fallen woman. "*Fuck you, bitch!*"

Dani couldn't breathe, couldn't move, the pressure in her chest was overwhelming, crippling her every living instinct. Pain spooled throughout her battered body, her veins ignited with blistering agony and her teeth tingled, her lungs ached for glorious release. The first flames of instinctual panic began to ignite at the base of her brain.

She thought she was going to die.

Her right hand slapped at the bulletproof vest and felt the lead embedded in the Kevlar, the bruising a dull ache beneath, the black blemish already beginning to form on her left breast. The same hand sprawled to the carpet, blindly searching for her Beretta, her only chance of survival. Her left arm, coated in blood, began to tremble and twitch.

*Don't die, sis. Don't die.*

Dani heard Teddy's voice in her mind, but couldn't remember where from, probably a videogame or something. One of the many cherished memories she'd tried so hard to forget.

*Don't die.*

Or was she on the verge of death, was she receiving a second chance?

*Don't die. Dobber dobber boffin –*

Finally, the air escaped her lungs in a whoosh, making her gasp loudly. She slowly rolled over and pushed herself up, grunting, ignoring the absolute agony rippling through her chest and arm.

Furlong narrowed his eyes. "You gotta be fucking kidding me?"

As if witnessing a miracle, the men watched in awe as Dani staggered to her feet, her crippled arm pinned to her side, blood dripping from her numb fingertips. Her legs were uneasy, wobbly, her dark clothing hiding the ceased trajectory of the bullet. Her right arm held a Beretta uneasily against her leg.

Furlong pulled his pistol and aimed. "Why won't you fucking die?"

Dani grinned and pointed her weapon. "Why don't...you...why don't you tell them how you helped me?"

Furlong paled, the blood rushing from his face. "Wh...what are you talking about?"

"Tell them. You led them into this ambush; you did it because I told you. You betrayed your boss," she uttered, a dribble of blood slipping from her lips. She looked beyond Furlong, goading the other soldiers. "He sold you out, lads."

The four men looked at one another quizzically. Furlong span slowly, his face still throbbing from the broken cheekbone, his heart pulsing through every inch of his terrified body. He held up a hand in surrender. "Don't listen to her, guys."

The four men nodded, looking down the hall at their fallen comrades, and then stared at Furlong. Dani closed her eyes and breathed deep, blocking out the throbbing agony. Ignoring the sweat and burning pain, she stumbled forward, leaning against the wall, pushing away from Furlong. Away from the line of fire.

Seconds later, the four men unloaded on Furlong with their weapons, gunning him down in cold blood. Portions of ragged flesh spiraled from his corpse as he flopped and spun on the spot, the bullets tearing chunks from his body.

His destroyed left arm slopped to the ground beneath the unforgiving blow of a shotgun blast, squelching as the red fluid sprayed from the shredded stump. The exposed, broken bone stuck in the carpet, pinning the arm at a sickening angle. Furlong howled as his life sprayed from his body in a hail of brutal gunfire.

Dani lined up the shot and killed the nearest soldier, the bullet mashing through his eye. He collapsed backwards, plunging into his colleagues. The four men stumbled, their weapons knocked to the ground, bullets still spewing. Furlong's bloody body, the skin merely a montage of blood and shredded gore, slumped to its knees. Dani hoisted herself from the wall with a grunt and stood behind him, shoving her injured arm into a fist-sized hole in his back, forming a human shield. Pain screamed up her shoulder as she lifted the injured limb, but she felt the adrenaline slowly kicking in.

*Kill or be killed.*

Grimacing, she pushed forward, sending the corpse into the soldiers. One fired from the ground, taking Furlong's head clean off, the severed neck muscles no longer supporting it. The blood-soaked skull ricocheted into the air, arced and bounced down the hallway like a football. Dani emerged from behind the headless corpse and fired, killing the second soldier with a double tap to the chest. With startling precision, she shot the remaining soldiers in the head and collapsed to the floor. The splatter of brain and bone filled the air as the violence came to a halt.

Opening her eyes, breathing into the rough carpet, Dani felt an overwhelming urge to vomit. Her battered body throbbed; her left arm – now coated in Furlong's entrails – was totally numb and she was slowly losing a lot of blood. With reckless abandon and irritation, she unzipped her hoody and tossed it aside.

She then wrenched the strap of her bulletproof vest, dropping the compromised armour to the ground. She winced and groaned. She slid her good hand beneath her skintight top and gently touched the bruise above her left nipple. The skin was soft, tender.

Her hazy eyes fell to her bloody arm. The skin, ragged and dark crimson beneath the sleeve, oozed blood freely. The sound of a bloody pitter-patter from her fingertips made her groan.

*Fuck*, she thought.

*This is going to kill me.*

Scooping the hoodie from the floor, she wrapped it around her arm, tying the sleeves tight against the bullet groove. It wasn't the best dressing, but it would do. With the slight pressure applied, she found she could move it a little easier. She picked up the bulletproof vest and slipped it over her head and on to her shoulders, not tying the waist straps. The armour, though compromised, would still be better than the thin cotton that currently covered her battered body.

For the first time, Dani realised that death was a formality, almost a certainty.

She closed her eyes once more.

*You have nothing to lose.*

She opened them and glanced at the wooden double doors before her.

The nameplate read *Ross Rhodes – CEO*.

She smiled; her crimson-specked teeth forming a hideous, malicious grin beneath a visage peppered with gun residue and spilt blood.

*The moment of truth.*

Dani walked forward, gun cocked, ready for anything, including death.

*It's almost over.*

# TWENTY

Scott glanced steadily around the lobby, observing the bloody massacre before him. Howes, inexperienced in such fieldwork, held a hand to her mouth to stifle a scream or potential vomit, her eyes wide in absolute horror. The acrid stench of sulphur, blood and death made her eyes water.

Scott checked all three bodies. "Male, all wearing similar outfits. Expensive suits, matching shoes, carrying firearms. Whoever did this was good, precise. Two shots per person, no double taps." Scott tapped their chests gently with a knuckle. "No bulletproof vests." He gazed high and wide, scanning the entire room for damage. "No stray shots. This was done quickly and efficiently."

Howes grimaced as she walked over. "Still think your girl did this?"

Scott shook his head. "No, this was done by someone with firearms experience."

"A year is a long time," Howes interjected.

"Meaning?"

"She could have had lessons, taught herself. Even in London, that shit goes down everywhere. I've been to a few illegal ranges myself, closed some down."

Scott nodded, agreeing with his colleague.

"What shall we do?"

Scott rubbed his face. "Call backup. Get armed response down here. I think the carnage is just beginning."

*****

A second bullet thudded into the open door, chipping away shards of polished wood. They fell to the carpet harmlessly. Dani sighed, stood behind the second of the double doors, itself closed and reinforced, something confirmed by several bullets thudding harmlessly against the other side. She could feel the vibrations trembling up her back.

Silence filled the hallway, the tension paired with the stench of sulphur and body odor in the musty air. The sweat trickling down her back and sides, the slick nape of her neck, her soggy hair – they were all commonplace now, Dani blocked them out. The pain rocking her injured arm had started to subside, the occasional spike of agony forced her to grit her teeth and curse loudly.

It didn't matter. They knew she was there.

"I'm here for Ross Rhodes."

A bullet screamed into the carpet, puffing black shreds of nylon and polyester into the air. No one said anything. Dani suspected that Rhodes would have an A-team as such, dedicated, trained soldiers who existed solely for his protection detail. Unlike the soldiers she'd faced thus far, these were a lot more organised, taking up a formidable position, one easily and safely defended against a vengeful teenager.

Dani patted her waist, her trembling fingers tracing the contours of her ammo belt, a thin strap of plastic stitched with small pockets. Previously hidden beneath her hoodie, which now acted as a makeshift tourniquet on her bullet-shattered arm, she felt the familiar metal rims of several magazines. Three pockets were empty because of her shooting thus far. After finding what she wanted, she nodded to herself.

"I'm here for Ross Rhodes," she repeated.

Still, she heard nothing. The audible sound of breathing was faint on the air. Remembering the images on the monitors, she knew that three people stood between her and Rhodes. Three people intent on waiting her out.

She spat on the carpet, the phlegm pink with blood. The movement agitated her arm, made her wince. Despite the makeshift tourniquet, the blood was soaking through and beginning to drip from her fingers once more.

She knew she didn't have much time. Waiting wouldn't benefit her.

"If you let me through, I'll let you live," she goaded, her breath starting to rasp. Dani shook her head groggily, and dug her good fingers into her leg, drawing an ounce of pain to spur her on. "My business is with your boss."

"The only way you're leaving here is in a body bag." The taunt was final, clerical. These people meant business.

Dani smiled. "Have it your way."

She slipped a hand grenade from her belt and stared at the green sphere, trying to remember how it worked. Pull the pin, flick the spoon off and toss. Simple enough. The woman looked down at her torn, bloody arm and sighed. She placed the pin between her teeth and yanked with her good hand. Her teeth groaned and creaked with the pressure of the grip, the pin slowly easing away from the device. After a few seconds, the pin squeezed loose with a metallic screech. She spat it out and held the device before her, flicking the spoon with her thumb. It rang loudly, flicking off the grenade, bouncing to the carpet below.

"You had this coming," she uttered, and tossed the grenade around the door. Dropping to a crouch, she shoved into the corner formed between the protective door and the wall.

Dani heard the grenade bounce off a wooden surface. Screams immediately rang from the room, panic and fear overwhelming the soldiers.

"*Grenade!*"

"*What the fuck?*"

"*Where is it?*"

"It bounced over there."

"*Grab it, toss it back.*"

"Fuck that…get down."

An explosion rocked the hallway, sprawling Dani to the floor, the blast blowing the door off its hinges and launching it down the corridor, inches above her head. It crashed into a window, cracking the glass. Immense heat filled the hallway and Dani yelled, the sound lost on the force of the explosion. Dani felt herself passing out from the heat and exertion, her crippled arm pounding spikes of agony into her weakened brain.

She closed her eyes.

\*\*\*\*\*

Sowder groaned loudly and coughed, spraying dark blood down her front, the red fluid dribbling from her lips. Every inch of her skin burned and sizzled, her hair felt like it was made of lava. She opened her eyes and immediately closed them, blocking out the bright flames before her. Blindly, she patted her outfit, her arms and legs, testing for rogue flames.

There were none. She was okay; the heat causing her discomfort was from a different source. Fingering the floor, she rolled over onto her front, groaned, and opened her eyes again, this time under the protection of darkness provided by her body.

Opening her eyes welcomed her to a new level of hell.

As if clearing a distorted signal, her ears began to function again. She heard the sizzling of various materials, scorched and destroyed by the blast of the device…a hand grenade. She heard wood creaking, various structures compromised by the annihilation caused by the weapon.

*What the fuck is that bitch doing with a hand grenade?*

The entire room was a collage of deep reds, casual oranges and bright yellows, the three shades providing a pleasant, attractive colour to the obvious devastation that surrounded her. Shoving a shattered chair from her leg, she stood up, hobbling from behind the desk that had saved her life. As she rose, she noticed the desk was nothing more than a charred mess, the lapping flames from a stray, destroyed monitor working on its surface. The air was thick with dark smoke and she coughed, dropping to a crouch to avoid the deadly mist.

Rinaldi's exposed skull greeted her as she dropped, her knee squelching in the splattered brains of her comrade. His face had disintegrated in the explosion, his face no more, the front of his skull a cracked opening that allowed the charred cerebral matter and sinew to flow to the carpet freely. His hair, or what remained of it, burned, filling the immediate space with a noxious smell, one that soon dispersed on the heat of the overall destruction. The remainder of his body lay crippled beneath collapsed ceiling tiles and an overturned, burning desk. The telephone transformed before her very eyes, became an oozing puddle of black plastic that dripped onto his scorched flesh.

Sowder retched, crawling away from her fallen friend. She scoured the room for Gilson and didn't see him anywhere. As the smoke began to clear, the explosion no longer ringing in her ears, she saw a shattered arm sticking out from a black mess of wood and concrete. The wall had collapsed inwards, crushing Gilson beneath it. His broken arm, the skin seared and bubbling, lay upturned, the bloody fingers grasping at nothing. The shattered radius protruded through the flesh, the bloody skin stretched and torn on its sharp point.

She tried to imagine the trajectory of the device and realised it must have bounced off the desk before her and rolled into the corner, obliterating Gilson and the surrounding wall. She was surprised that any part of his body had 'survived.'

The question returned again.

*What the fuck is that bitch doing with a hand grenade?*

Bradley had a lot to answer for.

*Just a teenager my arse.*

Sowder winced, her bruised leg nearly collapsing beneath her. She ambled past the desk, seeking the bright opening of the hallway, the doors no longer hooked to the hinges. Reaching to her waist, she pulled her pistol from its holster.

*Where the fuck are you?*

Stumbling through the demolished doors, Sowder squinted, the smoke receding somewhat. Small pieces of flaming wood peppered the carpet like misshaped candles. The blackened carpet in the doorway burned, wisps of smoke curling from the singed fibres, the grey tiling beneath showing through. She stepped over it.

Halfway down the hallway, at the crux of the corner, she saw a woman crawling away. She lay on her front, her left arm inert by her side, the right arm working hard to pull her away from the heat. Light from a nearby window shone down on her, showing the extent of her injuries. A blood-soaked hoodie lay strewn on the carpet behind her. Sowder smiled, realising she had a prime advantage. She holstered her weapon slowly.

*I'm going to enjoy this.*

Sowder hobbled forward and leant down, grabbing the woman by her damaged arm. Dani screamed in agony and rolled over, kicking Sowder in the stomach, partially winding her. Sowder lurched backwards, landing on her rump. Dani struggled to her feet slowly, her arm still inert, her weary eyes glazing over.

Sowder looked at the teenager and smiled, impressed. "I have to give it to you, you got this far. Not bad for a kid."

Dani said nothing.

"On another day, I might even offer you a job. Thing is, you just killed two of my friends, absolutely massacred them. Who throws a hand grenade into a gunfight? What a lack of fucking respect."

Dani wobbled awkwardly, her legs weak beneath her unbalanced weight. Again, she said nothing.

"Not much of a talker, eh?"

The air began to clear, the fresh air from the cracked window filtering the acrid smoke from the room. Sowder narrowed her eyes and noticed the scars, the wounds on Dani's face highlighted by the natural light spiking through the glass behind her. She shook her head. "Damn. You really aren't having a good day."

With that Sowder charged, her head low, her arms wide. Dani saw it coming and lifted a knee, ramming the tough bone into Sowder's face. Her nose exploded, blood and bone sliding across her sweaty, sooty cheeks. Sowder staggered back, coughing loudly.

Dani didn't wait.

She stepped forward and hooked her arm around Sowder's neck, grasping the woman in a front facelock. Pulling upwards, pressing her forearms into the woman's neck, Sowder began to choke as Dani applied leverage to her throat. The female soldier began to flap, her arms slapping at thin air in an attempt to push Dani off her, to no avail. Dani glanced behind her and grinned, moving backwards, dragging the woman's unbalanced weight with her.

"I'm not much of a talker, but actions speak louder than words."

Dani hoisted Sowder to her feet and launched her against the window. She hit the glass with a thud, which soon followed with a loud, splintering crack. For indeterminable seconds, Sowder found gravity holding her, balancing her body in the air, the fragile glass supporting her weight. "No, no...no," she found herself saying, her arms outstretched to spread her weight.

Dani stepped forward. "Yes."

She collected the Beretta from the carpet and fired several times, the bullets hammering into the woman's chest and shoulder. The bullets piled through, spraying blood and tissue against the glass, shattering the already fragile window. The glass began to fall away in rivulets, glittering in the emerging morning sun as they dropped silently to the street below. Dani leaned in close and sneered, blood and sweat dripping from her face.

"I told you, I wanted Rhodes, that you didn't have to die, but you didn't fucking listen."

She punched Sowder in the face, smashing hot vermilion across the glass, and kicked the woman, finally breaking the webbed pane behind her. Sowder screamed as she found herself falling, ejected through the empty pane into the chilly air. Her scream dwindled as she hurtled to the street forty stories below.

Dani fell to one knee and gasped, holding her chest. The cool air soothed her face and she closed her eyes. Mustering all of her strength, she straightened up, checked the ammunition on her Beretta, collected her weapons bag, and struggled down the hallway, passing through the shattered wooden doors. The fire warmed her skin as she walked, navigating the carnage, the subsiding flames harmlessly dancing on the furniture. Walking through the destroyed room, she came to a final set of double doors, embroidered with massive gold letters. *RR.*

Shooting the handle, the lock shattered and clunked to the floor. She kicked the doors open and stepped through, screaming as she did. The bloody, battered woman emerged in a vast office, one minimal in décor, the centerpiece being a huge oak desk backed against a wall seemingly made of glass. She realised it was one huge window, which provided an exquisite view of London. The room smelled clean, with a hint of bourbon in the air.

The leather chair behind the desk swivelled around to reveal a man with slick black hair and a scar on his forehead. A smile spread across his face, the flesh pockmarked with deep acne scars and decorated with a dishevelled beard.

His hands interlaced before him, his elbows positioning them in front of his face.

The leer was one of utter confidence and power.

Dani coughed. "Ross Rhodes?"

The man nodded. "You must be Dani? I heard so much about you."

"I'm here to kill you," Dani spat, her body wavering with exhaustion and blood loss.

"I'm impressed you got this far. But, you didn't think it was going to be this easy, did you?"

Dani's eyes exploded with bright light as a blow from her left knocked her to the tiled floor. She collapsed easily and slid a few feet, her balance compromised and her brain rattling in her skull. Her weapons bag slid across the ground behind her. Landing on her face, she groaned, blood and saliva drooling from her lips. Her head pounded, her heartbeat throbbed throughout every inch of her body. She probed her teeth with her tongue and felt a tooth snap from the root.

Turning over, she saw a hulking brute of a man step from the shadows and crack his knuckles. Her glazed eyes failed her, recognition not imminent, until the man spoke. He smiled at the fallen woman. "So, we meet again."

Dani's eyes widened.

In all the commotion, in her determination to find Rhodes, she'd misplaced Bradley. Cursing herself internally, she pushed herself to her feet. Bradley sidestepped, keeping the woman at a safe distance. "So, you found me, found us?"

Dani wiped her lips with a forearm and nodded. "I have my ways."

Bradley smiled. "A promise is a promise, I suppose."

Dani staggered backwards. "It's over. For both of you."

Bradley glanced at Rhodes, who simply chuckled. He poured himself a measure of bourbon and flicked his hands in their direction. "Kill the bitch; she's wasted enough of my time."

Bradley turned towards Dani, laughing. "I see you didn't lose your smile."

"You didn't lose your sense of humour...wait, no, you never had one."

Bradley chuckled again.

"You have a lot of fight in you, kid. It's going to be a shame to waste you."

Dani put her left arm out and leaned on the wall, white fire and pain and suffering whipping up her spine, her aching, battered body tingling and throbbing, on the verge of shutdown. Her mind was a muddle of partial images.

Bradley in his balaclava, cutting her face, killing her brother – the images forced themselves back into her mind's eye. The images built and ignited a rage deep within, turned into a focused mentality. Her brother's voice, distorted and deep, then fast and high-pitched, inspired her, spurred her on.

She didn't have long.

But, with Bradley, she wanted him done quickly.

Bradley stepped forward, a boot clonking on the pristine tiles. "You ready to die, Danielle?"

Dani slumped to her knees, her blood-soaked chin low. Bradley laughed, mocking the teenager with a pointed finger. "She can't even stand up. I've been waiting a year to do this, it's going to be so easy. Rhodes, promise me I can fuck the body when I'm done?"

"You kill her and you can do whatever you fucking want with her," his boss replied, sipping his bourbon. "Why do I hire these people?" He added.

Reaching down into her black bag, Dani lifted the SPAS 12 shotgun and cocked it, the heart-wrenching *snick snack* filling the room with dread, putting everyone on notice.

Including Bradley, who turned with a wide glare, disbelief in his frightened eyes.

"I've been waiting a year too, but it's over. Right now. This is for Teddy and my mother, you cunt."

Dani fired.

A shotgun fires metallic buckshot, a shell containing multiple spherical objects that spread as it fires, widening the blast radius and causing massive, severe blunt trauma. Bradley stood four feet from Dani as she lifted the weapon and pulled the trigger, his stance bringing him closer to the seemingly defenceless teenager.

His face ignited with the blast, his eyebrows catching fire and the skin shearing away, shredded into a blood pulp. The concentrated buckshot stove in his massive forehead and mushed his eyes before pulverising the bone at the top of his skull. His scalp, hair still attached, exploded from his head, and twirled across the office, smacking the tiles with a soggy splat.

Sticky globs of brain and sinew hung from the neck stump, with many more splattering against the floor.

Bradley's bloody corpse toppled forward and landed an inch from Dani, the blood spraying from his body sluicing onto her face.

She didn't care.

Dani stood up and reloaded.

*Snick snack.*

Rhodes, who was watching the events unfold, dropped his tumbler, the glass smashing on the desk and spilling amber liquid down his front. Dani stumbled across the office, with all the resemblance of the undead in a cheap horror movie, and aimed the shotgun at the gangland boss. Rhodes, who wasn't armed, pushed the chair back and retreated, heading for a locker behind him. His left hand fumbled for a bundle of keys in his trouser pocket.

"Now, now. Don't be hasty, let's talk this through."

Dani chuckled, a half-hearted noise that escaped her lips.

Blood trickled down her face, the left scar had reopened, the flesh hung loose in two torn flaps. She watched Rhodes retreat and followed him slowly, in no hurry. "There will be no talking. You killed my family. My father worked for you in good faith and you rewarded him by murdering him, murdering my mother and my kid brother."

"Nothing personal, Danielle. It was just business."

"My father called me Danielle, you don't fucking get to call me that. Because of you, I lost everything, my life was destroyed." She bashed the stock of the shotgun against her face, opening the scar more. She felt warm blood adding to her already crimson face. "I dreamt of this moment for over a year, every night and every fucking second of the day. I wondered what I would say given the chance, if I would say anything, if I would even get this far. My mind worked on this plan non-stop, during sleep, during showers, during weapons training. It was constant, my way of life."

Rhodes found his keys and turned, pushing the handle of the locker down.

It stayed firm, locked. Rhodes cursed and searched through the keys, trying to find the right one. "I suppose I should be honoured you decided to come here personally."

Dani continued her approach. "Now I'm here, I see you're nothing but a common criminal, a man who pays for death and results, a man who thinks the law doesn't apply to him. A coward hiding behind a small, personal army because he doesn't have the balls to do anything himself."

"Fuck you, bitch. I ain't no coward."

"No? In my eyes, you're avoiding a fight with a teenager. That makes you a fucking pussy. Well, the moment I saw my brother's head split apart like a melon, I swore this day would come. And I'll be damned if anyone is going to stop me."

Dani tossed the shotgun aside. She drew her Beretta and aimed at Rhodes. "This is for Teddy and my mother...and my father."

Dani fired.

The bullet *whupped* across the office and pulverised Rhode's leg. His kneecap imploded, spraying blood, bone and shredded fabric to the floor. Rhodes screamed and collapsed backwards, the keys falling from his grasp and tinkling on the tiled floor. They slid under his desk.

Dani walked closer and stood over Rhodes, her Beretta aimed at his face. The gangland boss cowered, his hands before his face, his leg a gory mess, muscle and blood prolapsed onto the ground beneath him.

A pool of blood began to form around him.

Dani stared, her eyes wet with anger. Tears rolled down her cheeks, cutting a clean swathe through the drying blood. Her hand gripped the gun so tight that it shook violently, her knuckles white. Images of her family flicked through her brain like a swift slideshow. She blinked, the action spilling warm tears to her chest. They plinked and exploded as they made contact.

Rhodes sneered. "Fucking coward, you don't have the balls."

Dani hesitated.

"If you kill me, someone else will take over. I have dozens of men who will happily step into my shoes. Then, you're fucked. They will want revenge. They will fucking find you, you *cunt*. You thought that Chelsea grin was horrible…wait until they get a hold of you and violate you over and over. Some of them don't possess Bradley's restraint. You're dead, you're fucking dead."

"Dani?"

The mention of her name stopped Dani in her tracks. Keeping the Beretta aimed at Rhodes, she began to turn.

"Dani?"

She glanced towards the door. DCI Scott stepped through the entrance, dressed in a bulletproof vest and brandishing a MPK5 machine gun, the standard issue firearm of the Armed Response Police, who followed a few steps behind. He had the weapon pointed at her in a defensive stance. "Dani, I need you to back away from Mr Rhodes."

Dani said nothing, didn't respond.

Rhodes began to chuckle.

"Fuck you, copper, Mr Rhodes was my father and he was a cunt. I want to make a complaint about this woman, she broke into my building and killed my men and was about to kill me before you came in."

Scott, his eye peering down the barrel of his weapon, glanced at Dani. His heart sunk, his mind spiralling. Dani took a small step backwards; her soggy eyes pinned on him.

He breathed out slowly.

*What happened to her?*

The left side of her head was matted, the blood a dark brown on her neck and shoulder, pinning her hair down. Her face was a mottle of bruises and scrapes, blood and abrasions, the scar on the left side of her face was open, the skin flapping. Her left arm hung limp, the fingers curled inwards, the flesh stained black with soot. A nasty bullet groove in the bicep still oozed red fluid and as she moved, the arm remained inert by her side. Her eyes were petrified, sanity all but lost within.

The Beretta in her right hand wavered, the barrel still pointing at Rhodes.

"Dani, I need you to put the gun down."

In his peripheral vision, DI Howes began to enter the room, followed by several armed response officers armed with MP5K machine guns. Scott held his hand out, beckoning them to stay put and out of sight, as not to worry the girl before him, one who was a shadow of her former self. Even as she watched him intently, he wondered if she was the same person, her gaze reminded him of a lion eyeing a gazelle.

"Do it, Danielle! Go on, you failed. You're a *fucking* failure, just like your cunt father and your whore mother."

Dani trembled, looking from one man to another, torn between two decisions. The gun didn't lower. Scott shook his head, "Dani, if you use that weapon, we will have to take you down. Please don't make me do that."

"Yeah, Dani. Don't let the filth take you down. That's the most humiliating thing anyone can suffer. Mind you, I want to see it. It'll be a keepsake, the failure of an entire family. Do it, *do it*!"

Dani tossed the weapon aside. It thudded against the wall and came to a rest. She placed her right hand in the air, not even lifting her left hand.

Scott nodded. "You don't need to put your hands up, but I need you to step away."

Dani backed off, slowly, haphazardly. She stumbled and leaned on the desk, her body on the verge of shutdown. She grimaced, blood spooling from her mouth. "Ross Rhodes…"

"I didn't do anything, officer. Never trust the word of a psychotic bitch, they're all crazy."

"Shut up, Rhodes," Scott spat, his eyes still on Dani.

"Rhodes…he killed my pare…killed my family."

Scott nodded. "Okay."

"I want my solicitor," Rhodes spat.

Dani stumbled forward, her eyes closing. As blackness swallowed her, she saw Scott lurch forward to catch her.

Then, all was dark.

# TWENTY - ONE

Looking at the fallen woman, DCI Scott was caught in two minds. Brandishing a set of handcuffs from his belt, he moved towards Dani and paused. There was no doubt the violent carnage in the building was orchestrated by her, and a result of her bloody quest for revenge. The evidence all pointed to Dani, from the unfound fingerprints and DNA, to CCTV footage and Rhodes himself.

Still in shock and awe – *how could this quiet, mundane teenager commit such a violent act* – Scott remained indecisive. DI Howes entered the room on his command, the armed response officers surrounding her, monitoring Rhodes.

"Get off me, put me down," Rhodes said. Howes stepped in close. "Mr Rhodes, you have the right to remain silent…"

"Save me the lecture, sugar tits. I've heard it all before."

"I have to read you your rights, sir."

"Fuck my rights."

Rhodes spat in Howes' face, the sputum smacking her below the eye. She yelped, backing off. Rhodes smiled. "There's more where that came from, if you get my drift?" Rhodes began gyrating towards her. "Loads more!"

Scott looked over to Howes, who wiped the spit from her face. "Shut him up, DI, please."

Howes smiled, turned and kicked Rhodes in the groin, dropping the man to his knees, his arms hoisted by two officers. Silent and gasping from the pain, he become manageable.

"Get that piece of shit out of here," Scott commanded, staring down at Dani. "Read his rights to him in the fucking van."

The officers moved Rhodes from the room, taking the gangland boss into custody. Howes walked over, wiping her face with her sleeve. "Sorry, sir. I got carried away."

"No problem. Cunt had it coming."

Howes nodded, looking down at Dani. "Poor thing. He did this…I mean, Rhodes did that to her?"

"He was involved. I don't have the exact details yet."

"Fuck me," she uttered. "Evil knows no bounds. What you going to do with her?"

"Take her in. She can't be allowed to get away with this."

"She did us a huge favour. You can bring the underworld to its knees with Rhodes in custody, if you can make the crimes stick."

"I can. Murder, extortion, prostitution. We'll have to clean out the police too, remove all the bent coppers. Regardless, I don't think a visit from London's finest was on Rhodes' agenda today. I bet you find allsorts in that laptop and those drawers," he said, pointing to the desk. "We really caught him with his pants down."

Howes nodded. "I'll get forensics in, give it a proper examination."

"Yes, and get them to clear the bodies. I don't want anyone up here until it's done." Howes nodded and walked out of the room, leaving Scott alone with Dani.

He kneeled down, his gloved hand caressing her cheek. "What did they do to you?"

"Nothing I can't handle."

"Wha –"

Dani's right hand gripped Scott's forearm and pulled it close to her chest. She looped her legs around the arm, pulling the limb between her thighs, bending it at the elbow, and crossed her calves beneath his chin.

Scott began to gasp as Dani choked the DCI out.

His arm pinned, he attempted to swat at Dani with his free arm, but couldn't find any give with her legs pinning his shoulders in place.

"I'm sorry, DCI Scott, but I can't let you take me in."

"Dani…Dan…urgh…"

"It's nothing personal, but my work isn't done."

Scott began to fade. Dani watched the door, alert for any approaching police officers. Scott flopped, his arm limp at his side. Dani held on for a little longer and placed the unconscious DCI to the ground. She bent down, brushed a strand of bloody hair from her face, and kissed him on the forehead, leaving a red mark. "I'm sorry, Jack. Please forgive me."

Dani stood up and limped behind the desk, her left arm still dangling by her side. Finding the laptop, she disconnected the cables from its sockets and walked to the black bag, scooping up the shotgun as she went. She placed both items in the bag and zipped it shut.

Dani slung the bag over her right shoulder, wincing as it clattered against her back, and ambled towards the exit. Peering around the door, she spotted an empty hallway. The flames had subsided, the broken furniture and corpses placed like grotesque statues. The smell of charred wood and flesh was strong in the air.

Dani slowly walked forward, her destination being the black double doors by the shattered window. The doors were still closed. As she neared the bend, she listened intently. She heard nothing, sensed no one.

Reaching the doors, her hair fluttering on the chilly wind from the window, she opened them and slipped inside, closing them behind her.

She emerged in a huge, picturesque boardroom with a grand table in its centre, flanked by twenty chairs. In the middle of the table was a triangle speaker, the wood shining from a fresh coat of varnish. Dani ignored it and walked past, finding another door at the end.

Opening it, silence greeted her. The air was stale and warm, unfiltered, a strong scent of pungent plastic made Dani wrinkle her nose. No one had been in the room for some time.

The space was a receptionist office, unused, indicated by the plastic wrappings on the furniture. Placing the bag on the table, Dani removed a bottle of water and some plasters. Then, she took a swig and swallowed carefully, sighing in pleasure. She poured some of the liquid onto her injured arm, washing the bullet wound, hissing through bared teeth. The dried blood began to wash and flake away.

Happy, she poured the remainder of the bottle over her head and face. Dropping the bottle to the floor, she slipped a towel from the bag and wiped her arm gently. Cleaner, she scrubbed her face slowly, removing the blood. She then stuck four plasters along the opened scar in her face, hooking the fleshy flaps together carefully. Removing a third, smaller towel, she wrapped it around her arm and tied it tightly, pushing on the wound. She then removed a second black hoodie from the bag and carefully slid it over her left arm, wincing as she did. She slipped her right arm in, zipped it up and pulled the hood over her head. To finish the outfit, she wrapped a snood around her face tightly, tucking it in, covering the scars and ensuring the ruptured wound stayed closed. As a temporary fix, it would do.

Turning around, she glanced in a mirror.

*No longer a bloody mess. Just a regular Joe from the gym.*

Dani placed everything back in the bag, closed it and turned, walking to the freight elevator in the corner. Pushing the button, she waited for the doors to open, slipped in and disappeared.

*****

"Scott, *Scott!*"

DCI Scott sat up, coughing. His throat felt tender, his mind cloudy and floating. He tried to sit up and fell sideways. DI Howes lifted him by an arm, supporting his weight with her frame. Scott shook his head, pushing the cobwebs from his mind.

"Where's Dani?" Howes asked.

"Fucked if I know. She...she…"

"What's this?" Howes wiped the blood from his forehead and mashed it between her fingertips. "Did she kiss you? It looks like lipstick."

"No, that's blood."

"No shit," Howes uttered, pulling a radio from her belt. "All officers, be on the lookout for a teenage girl, about five-nine, brown hair, pretty messy. Approach with caution and apprehend. Defining features are two large scars on her face, a Chelsea grin. She is armed and dangerous." Howes shut the radio off. Scott laughed, sitting down on the desk.

"You're pretty chipper for someone who just got assaulted," the DI said.

"She's probably long gone by now."

"We'll see."

"That's just it," Scott uttered, wiping his face. "I don't think we'll see her ever again."

*****

*There's so much wrong with this dark world, so much depravity in society.*

*We expect innocent people to live in a world that sees them attacked, assaulted, robbed, taking advantage of – all on a daily basis. Culprits are criminals, strangers, family members, and government corporations, all inspired and motivated by the one thing that corrupts us all.*

*Greed.*

*Old men mugged in the street for their measly pension. Women raped and violated because certain individuals get a sadistic kick out of such an activity. A cripple is evicted from his home because he can't keep up payments on his house, payments inflated annually by the very bank who offered him the loan, knowing full well his finances were ultimately restricted.*

*People beaten in the street.*

*Humans gunned down for no reason.*

*Women forced into prostitution.*

*Teenagers mutilated and left for dead.*

*I know a little about that last one. I lived through it after all.*

*I see the scum on the streets and it makes me sick to my stomach. I had my revenge because I was fortunate to do so. Others aren't so lucky, those who are unfortunate enough to fall foul of crime, those who are victims of everyday bad luck and disgusting human behavior.*

*Those people need someone. Someone who can have their back, someone who can fend for them in the way that is right, someone who can seek out those who did them wrong and exact some justice.*

*Those people need someone.*

*Those people deserve someone.*

*Those people have someone.*

*My name is Danielle.*

*I am Grin.*

69319286R00115

Made in the USA
Columbia, SC
19 April 2017